LESSER OF TWO EVILS

RORI BLEU

ROSIE CHAPEL

First printing: 2023
ISBN: 978-1-7635407-1-2 (eBook)
ISBN: 978-1-7635407-2-9 (Paperback)

Ulfire Pty. Ltd.
P.O. Box 1481
South Perth
WA 6951
Australia

Cover Design: R Norman
Cover Image: Canva/Deposit Photos
Designed in Canva
Internal images: Canva/Deposit Photos.
Created using appropriate licences.

✼ Created with Vellum

LESSER OF TWO EVILS

RORI BLEU

ROSIE CHAPEL

CHAPTER ONE

President Jamison Hyden was sequestered in the Oval Office watching videos of his past successes, all of which had culminated in his inauguration three years previously.

From the comfort of John F. Kennedy's rocking chair — an item of furniture, he had commandeered from the Smithsonian Museum's Presidential Exhibition, the day he assumed residency of the White House — he basked in the boisterous revelry of Americans celebrating his landslide victory.

While his opponents chalked up his win as little more than riding the skirts of his predecessor, Hyden deluded himself into believing, it was in appreciation of a lifetime dedicated to the people of the United States, which had encouraged them to conclude he was owed the position.

In truth, he was only now coming to grips with the fact, he had been in the right place at the right time. The three-term senator from Florida had filled a need for the Democrats as the VP on a ticket which featured the first openly lesbian woman as the party's flag bearer.

President Gwyneth Rollins had won her nomination easily, in part because she was willing to carry the elderly, white Southerner. The party leadership felt her staunch liberal views might deter the older population, and begged her to accept Hyden as the counterbalanced view. He was packaged to the electorate as a Conservative-leaning Centrist.

It led to interesting discussions, not only on the campaign trail, but also during televised talk shows. Representing both sides of the same coin, the duo debated the issues openly, effectively locking out the opposition party before coming to a unified front.

That was the dog and pony show the Democratic National Committee expected Hyden to abide by. He had no actual say in any decisions… either domestic or foreign.

In reality, the de facto Vice President was Rollins's wife Abigail, who flew around the world with her spouse. Outwardly, the image of the demure First Lady.

When international events required arm twisting with a velvet glove, it was Abigail who made a personal appearance in whichever country needed persuading. Fluent in several languages, including French, Farsi and Russian, her diction was elegant and captivating.

She had founded her own NGO to provide international medical and food relief, serving as its chairperson to ensure the supplies arrived to those in need, and remaining in that position until she stepped aside when her politically motivated mate decided to run for the Presidency.

A choice which enhanced Abigail's image as the devoted consort.

The foreign press loved her…almost as much as her wife… making it difficult for foreign leaders to refuse Abigail's audience or her requests in the name of the President.

The couple made an unstoppable and inseparable team, relegating Hyden to superfluous chores, particularly those requiring the presence of a male.

When the Rollinses hot-footed it to some war-torn country to negotiate a ceasefire between opposing warlords, Hyden was sent to Iowa to dangle subsidies, far below the market value, in front of hog farmers. The aim... to encourage them to halt their breeding program because the same *essential* ally needed to dump their livestock into the domestic market in order to bolster their emerging economy.

Similarly, while Rollins signed trade agreements lifting decades' long tariffs on Chinese steel, her Vice President was forced to face Pennsylvania steelworkers, promising a brighter future through the President's revitalization and re-education program. Keenly aware, their industry would collapse under the weight of cheaper imported steel, leaving their employees destitute.

None of this affected President Rollins's popularity because even though a small segment of America felt the impact of her policies, the majority benefited.

Construction companies were able to produce commercial and residential buildings at a more affordable rate, creating a boom in their industry, which resulted in an unprecedented gain in the real estate market.

The domestic hog breeders, who had opted to turn down the government man's offer, suffered because of the flood of foreign pork into the US, and countless stockyards went bankrupt.

The media were not interested in the misfortunes of a bunch of hicks in the Midwest. They lived in the flyover states which did not make the news... unless some picture-worthy natural disaster struck.

Besides, didn't pork come from grocery stores anyway?

Hyden's fingers did not directly affect Rollins's success, but the illusion of teamwork was all that mattered.

With Rollins's popularity at a record-high toward the end of her final term; bolstered by a strong economy and a successful foreign policy, the party heads felt certain Hyden would be a shoo-in to serve as her proxy for a third and possibly fourth term.

All he needed to do was continue with her programs, and the party was sure they would, at least, control the White House until Hyden decided to retire and write his memoirs. They had even hand-selected his running mate, a brash Latina, well versed in the concerns of America's failing immigration policies. At the time of her nomination, she was the youngest person to be elected as the Speaker of the House.

Hyden froze the image of the two standing on their party's platform at the convention in Philadelphia, their fingers interlocked and thrust into the shower of balloons and confetti.

A closer examination of the image confirmed what he had suspected all along, she was repulsed to be on the stage with him. There was a definite grimace on her face, almost certainly at being required to touch him.

He smirked, clearly she was a practitioner of the same mantra as he... *go along to get along.*

Vice President Estefanía Hernández preferred to work out of her office in the Eisenhower Executive Office Building, than her designated suite of rooms in the White House's

West Wing, so as to avoid being tarnished by Hyden's policies.

She had spent her incumbency building her future at the expense of the head of the party's ticket.

Through carefully cultivated contacts, developed while in Congress, she had managed to introduce legislation which eased the restrictions for citizenship for undocumented residents, effectively halting the practice of separating families, and accompanying accusations, by the most vocal of her own party, of *kids in cages.*

The fact, her party lost the House during the Presidential Election, did not stop her from working her magic.

Behind the scenes, she brought in the necessary votes, not only for the man who had assumed her position as Speaker — a member of the opposition party — but also to pass bills which increased the number of Border Patrol agents, and stiffened the penalties against the coyotes trafficking the desperate across the border.

It did not matter to Hernández that the credit for the passage of both bills went to others; she had won a more lucrative prize. The Speaker of the House *and* the House Minority Whip were now in her debt.

Which would prove very useful when she announced her run for the Presidency. To have the two men standing next to her on live television, definitely would not hurt her chances.

Hyden tossed the remote at the television, causing a number of LEDs to distort in the middle of the screen. He turned his back on the damaged unit, muttering, "Work a replacement into the next budget... maybe something larger in an 8K HD display. Nothing but the best for me, the current and future President."

Resuming his seat behind the Resolute Desk, he rubbed the bridge of his nose before picking up the *Post*. Above the fold, a photograph of the Republican candidates during their third round of debates.

While the paper's op-ed page agreed they offered nothing in the way of viable alternatives to the current administration's policy, what it *did* highlight was their unified and intense hatred of the current president.

Shaking his head in disgust, at this point he actually welcomed the weekly briefing provided by the FBI director Connor Sullivan.

The first file contained the comings and goings of his Vice President and, most assuredly, primary opponent, Estefania Hernández.

Hyden had kept close taps on Hernández, since the day she was sworn in, going as far as to have the FBI bug her office and screen her mail.

Scanning the phone records and abundance of emails, Hyden noted various names, *he* had used as donors during his run for the Oval Office, being contacted by his running mate… repeatedly… and more so after losing the Senate in the midterms.

While this was no surprise to Hyden, it annoyed him all the same because, it appeared, she was no longer attempting to mask her agenda.

Hyden was impressed with the quality of information, Sullivan had provided; proof he was a loyal toady. Sullivan had no problem bending, if not breaking the law for Hyden whenever a situation demanded.

"If that ungrateful bitch wants off the ticket, I'm sure Connor would jump at the chance to occupy the West Wing."

His perusal of the reports was interrupted by the buzz of his intercom.

Pressing the button, he answered without disguising the annoyance in his voice, "What is it, Margaret?"

"I'm sorry to disturb you, Mr. President…"

Margaret's decorum brought a smile to the old man's face; it was such a rarity these days. The press referred to him as Mr. Hyden, while the Republicans — and the majority of his own party — referred to him as the Crazy Old Man in the Oval Office.

"…Mr. Hutchinson is here and insists he sees you."

"Tell him I'm—"

"Jay, if you don't want to go back to selling shitty cars with questionable titles and histories, you'll see me now."

CHAPTER TWO

Minsk

Corporal John Wayne Davis woke from a restless sleep. His eyes shot to the door to make sure it was still secure, and then to the woman next to him.

He listened to the soft snoring of the prostitute, Gunny had foisted on him earlier when they were in the hotel bar.

Why is *she still here?* Davis had no idea.

The sex was pedestrian at best, exacerbating his irritation, given he did not want her company in the first place, but knew better than to refuse his Sergeant, and Gunny had *insisted*.

Something about a job well done.

The unsatisfactory copulation did nothing to alleviate the Iowan's consternation about what he had participated in during the last couple of days. Something he could not wrap his head around.

Sitting on the edge of the bed, he fumbled through the pocket trash on the nightstand, searching for his cigarettes.

His bedmate snorted and muttered something in Russian

or Belarusian, he had no idea which. It all sounded the same to him, and, anyway, whatever she was saying in her sleep sounded like a complaint about being disturbed.

Shaking his head, he could not believe she had fallen asleep before him.

"Just my luck."

Tiptoeing across the room, he opened the door to the narrow balcony and leaned against the railing. Lighting his cigarette, he looked out over the city of Minsk.

The urban sprawl made him long for the flowing farmland surrounding his home in Aplington, hunting deer or Canadian geese, instead of here.

Davis wondered, after what they had done, whether he would ever be allowed to return home.

His thoughts drifted back to the day at Camp Lejeune when he was summoned to his CO's office.

Three days previously
Camp Lejeune

Colonel Baxter looked up from the paperwork on his desk as the corporal entered and snapped to attention, giving him a sharp salute.

"At ease, Marine," Baxter said.

Davis noticed his Gunnery Sergeant was also in the office. A wave of unease swept through him, as he contemplated whether he was about to be reprimanded for some infraction he was unaware he had committed.

As usual, he could not read anything from Gunny's expression. The man always looked as though he was suffering from terminal constipation, pissed at the world because of it.

Baxter got straight to the point. "Marine, do you love your country?"

Davis barked the required response, "Sir, yes, sir."

"Can you follow orders without question?"

"Sir, yes, sir."

In retrospect, Davis wished he *had* questioned what the Colonial was asking of him but, being a good Marine over-rode wisdom.

"Word's come down that Gunny is being assigned to a mission out of country and will need a spotter. That's where you come in, Marine. Your scores in the field have been impressive. In fact, Gunny requested you specifically. You should consider it an honor."

"Sir, yes sir. Thank you, sir," Davis responded.

"You have fifteen to change into civvies and pack your belongings. Then report to the motor pool. The two of you will be flying out from OAJ on the government's dime.

"Now, get out of my office."

Saluting, Davis, turned to depart.

"One other thing, Marine."

Davis paused, his about face interrupted when Baxter said, "Your service weapon is to remain on base. You will be assigned a new one when you arrive at your duty station."

The corporal looked over his shoulder, unsure whether he should ask why, but Baxter preempted his query.

"Are you questioning an order, corporal?"

"No, sir."

Davis beat a hasty retreat to carry out the CO's commands.

The Bombardier Global 7500, which sat in the hangar at OAJ, known by the locals as Albert J. Ellis Airport, impressed the young Marine, as he and his Sergeant rolled up in the Hummer.

"Do ya reckon there's a cute stewardess aboard, Gunny?"

"Zip it, Davis," the Gunnery Sergeant ordered. "From here on out, you'll refer to me as Johnson."

Harking back to the conversation in Baxter's office, Davis assumed this was another of those orders, he was expected to obey without question.

Doing as his superior officer bade, Davis followed Johnson onto the jet.

His somewhat inexplicable yet growing resentment of the pending flight was exacerbated by the lack of flight attendants waiting to welcome him aboard, and escort him to his seat. Instead, he was greeted in the fuselage by a grizzled old man with a handheld metal detector.

While Johnson spoke to an equally surly woman, whom Davis assumed was the pilot, the man with the wand used it in a totally inappropriate manner, if he hoped to guarantee Davis was indeed unarmed.

Not satisfied with the efficacy of modern electronics, the old man was determined to perform a cavity search on the corporal. At this point, Johnson intervened to put a stop to it.

"Get your jollies some other time, Gus. Hustle your ass into the cockpit and help Chō get us off the ground."

"Are you kidding, Johnson," the old man grouched. "Last time, I tried to help her with anything, she threatened to toss my ass out of the plane at fifty thousand feet."

"Not my problem, Gus. Now git."

Straightening his clothes, Davis observed the way Johnson interacted with the older man, figuring they shared a long history.

Done talking to Gus, Johnson pushed passed Davis and headed to his seat at the rear of the jet.

Davis took the seat across the aisle.

Ignoring his junior non-com, Johnson removed a file from the folder, he had carried aboard, and began to read.

The jet rolled down the runway, gathered speed and took off, climbing quickly. Once they reached altitude, Davis attempted to open one of the blinds, to discover it was secured in place, permanently. He leaned forward to test the next couple, finding them in the same condition.

"Don't bother," Johnson said, without lifting his eyes from the file. "They're all like that. The CIA uses this craft for extraordinary renditions to their Black Sites. In fact, Osama Bin Laden was chained to the same—"

"Chained? Bin Laden was killed in his compound by Seal Team Six."

Johnson shook his head in disbelief at the Marine's naiveté. "Do you honestly believe, we would just shoot him and dump his body in the North Arabian Sea after administering the equivalent of last rights for Muslims?

"Hell, as we speak, the bastard's been shaved bald, head to toe, tied naked to some rafter suspended above a pit filled with pig shit, confessing to everything he's ever done in his life, and to things there's no way he was part of… like the assassination of Archduke Ferdinand precipitating World War One… for fear we will cut the rope."

Unable to discern whether Johnson was serious or not, Davis elected to change the topic.

"Can you at least tell me where we are heading?"

"Need to know, boy, and you don't need to know yet. So settle back and enjoy the flight."

Johnson tossed a nod to a cabinet at the front of the jet, "You might find something to drink up there, unless your new girlfriend, Gus, beat ya to it on the way to the cockpit.

"Now, shut it and let me do my work.

CHAPTER THREE

Vilnius, Lithuania
A private airport outside the city

Johnson jostled Davis from a sound sleep. "Wake up, Marine, we've landed."

Davis's head was fuzzy from dozing off shortly after drinking the whiskey he had found in the cabinet. He glanced at his watch trying to get his bearings, confused to see it read 20:37.

He put it to his ear to check whether it was functioning. The ticking of the sweep hand reassured him of that, but the time had him baffled.

Johnson explained, "I set your watch to local time already. We can't waste precious minutes while you dick around with that thing."

Rising to his feet and stretching, Davis replied, "Thanks," and followed Johnson out.

The two exited the jet into another hangar where a few men scurried about performing various tasks. No one paid any attention to the disembarking passengers, except the one who addressed Johnson.

He appeared to be in charge of operations.

The young Marine tried to eavesdrop on what the two were discussing, to be directed by Johnson to the black Defender truck with the soft top, its tailgate lowered in readiness.

"Climb in back," Johnson ordered Davis.

As Davis stepped up into the bed of the truck, he noted two boxes pushed against the back of the cab. He could not make out what was written on the wooden crates, but both bore the insignia of the Russian Armed Forces.

Taking a seat next to the crates, Davis was moved to speculate whether the men in the hangar were actually Russians, but given the distinct lack of uniforms, he could not be certain.

He listened to them calling out to each other, and they sounded like Americans.

Oh my God, this must be one of the Black Sites, Gunny referred to, Davis worried he was about to be dropped into some hole, never to be seen again.

Johnson finished his conversation and joined Davis in the back of the truck, closing and securing the flap behind him.

"Any chance you can tell me where we are and where we are headed to?"

"You don't need to know yet, Marine," was the unsatisfactory reply.

With an unexpected lurch, the truck took off for parts unknown.

Bug River
Belarus Side

Every twenty minutes or so, Davis checked his watch. Through the slit in the flaps, he could see it was still night and, occasionally, saw the flash of passing taillights. The truck stopped once, and that was for gas.

Davis had asked whether it was possible to stop so he could relieve himself, but Johnson kicked a bucket at him, saying, "Feel free."

After what felt like an eternity in the back of the uncomfortably bouncing truck, it came to a halt. Davis discerned the early morning sun bleeding through the flaps. He heard the doors of the cab open and shut, followed by the roar of another engine, then silence.

Confident they were alone, Johnson rose from his bench to inspect the Russian crates.

Opening the first, a wry smile curved his lips at the collection of Russian made MP-443 Grach pistols and their pre-loaded extended magazines, as well as half a dozen AN-94 Nikonov Assault Rifles.

Handing the sleek weapon to Davis, Johnson explained, "Be honored your government has granted you the use of one of these beauties. They're so expensive not even the Russian Military can afford to issue them."

Confused, Davis asked, "But why would they arm us with these rifles when we could have brought M4s, which is a much better—"

The look the Gunnery Sergeant shot the man over his shoulder told Davis his dissertation on weaponry was falling on deaf ears.

"Grab a pistol as well," Johnson instructed.

He closed the lid. "Help me move this bottom crate out of the truck."

Alighting into the sudden brightness, Davis blinked a couple of times, ducking to avoid being hit in the head by the box, Johnson was pushing across the bed.

Setting the crate on a grassy knoll beside the riverbank, Johnson opened it to reveal a number of Russian SPG-9 rockets.

Mimicking Johnson, Davis shaded his eyes to squint across the river to the other side. He could see a small village, its residents preparing for the new day.

At his wits' end trying to understand why they were here, he repeated, "Will you tell me now what we are doing here?"

Not answering, Johnson placed the rockets to the side, gingerly, then removed the tripod base and launcher for the rockets, stored at the bottom of the case.

The assembly of the firing system, complete, and before Davis could reiterate his question, Johnson spoke, "Guess there's no harm telling you now. A UN convoy will drive through the village with desperately needed supplies, and we are here to serve as their guardian angels."

"That's all well and good, sir, but why the secrecy, and why the Russian weapons?"

"You know there are countries in the UN who think the United States shouldn't be in this part of Europe, and that we are incapable of acting as Peacekeepers. So, we're here on the downlow, which is why I could not brief you earlier. I could not have you risk the success of the operation by telling your mom or girlfriend.

"Okay, Marine, grab an earpiece and take up position a klick that way…" Johnson nodded his head in the direction he wanted Davis to go, "…in case we get company."

His head swimming from the ludicrous story, Johnson had just fed him, Davis did as instructed, and hid in a convenient ditch. Weapon at the ready, he waited for whichever country's army to arrive in full battle mode.

That's when he heard it, the simultaneous fire of SPG-9s. Davis was not on scene when, it had to be, Johnson assembled the second.

Seconds later, explosions rang out from the opposite bank. Smoke and fire billowed skywards. Sirens and screams could be heard on their side of the river.

Pressing the transmit on his radio, Davis bawled, "Gunny, what did you—"

A high-pitched squeal cut off the rest of the transmission.

Hearing the muffle roar of truck's engine, Davis, sprinting as though the hounds of hell were chasing him, retraced his route along the track to where Gunny had parked.

Readying himself, he managed to grasp the rear handle, and haul himself into the back of the truck as Johnson raced by, convinced the violent action had dislocated his shoulder.

The two drove through the day, entering Minsk as the afternoon waned.

Minsk

Davis took another drag on his cigarette before flicking it over the balcony's railing. He stood motionless in the Minsk night breeze, wondering how far up the chain the orders for this massacre went.

Obviously, Baxter is in on it. I wonder if the Marine Commandant has any idea. Shit, if that's the case, the entire Joint Chiefs are probably party to it and, if that's true... surely...

Lost in thought, Davis failed to hear the door to his hotel room open and close. Deeming it time to kick the hooker out, Davis froze when a piercing pain radiated out from the base of his skull.

The reaction of whatever had been injected into his brain was immediate. Teetering on his feet, he saw a blurry image pointing something at the woman in the bed.

The flash from its end hurt Davis's eyes and the explosion which rang out deafened him.

Stumbling forwards, blindly intent on defending himself, he felt hands grab him, and the intruder shoved what Davis registered was a pistol into his hand. Before the young Marine could think of using it, he was toppled over the railing to the pathway six stories below.

CHAPTER FOUR

Washington, D.C.

Kira Monroe sat in her usual mid-section of the White House Press Corps seats, only half listening to the President's Press Secretary, Bill Foster, drone on about Hyden's upcoming campaign trip through the Rust Belt to shore up votes in the swing states of Ohio and Pennsylvania.

With her pedigree — great-granddaughter of famed war correspondent, Ted Monroe — Kira considered these mundane briefings beneath her.

Her dream was to lead a band of fearless, like-minded reporters, the way Ted did during World War Two.

His handful of skilled and courageous radio journalists were always in the thick of the battle, making sure to be embedded in frontline battalions. As for their boss, he braved the nightly rain of hell from the German Luftwaffe.

Against the backdrop of sirens wailing and the percussion of exploding bombs, he opened every broadcast in an unruffled manner, "Good evening, from the heart of terror."

Her father, Robert Monroe, had also answered the call,

transmitting the plight of humanity across the world. His restless nature prompted him to drag his family around the globe to report critical events such as the fall of the Berlin Wall, or the Afghan War from downtown Kabul, or Riyadh so he could sneak across the border with Yemen to expose widespread atrocities being inflicted in the prolonged and brutal conflict between warring factions.

Witnessing history firsthand, along with her father filling her head with his political views, spurred Kira to follow family tradition and major in journalism. Rather than attending college in the States, she elected to enrol at the Technical University Berlin, a city where she spent most of her childhood after Robert secured the position of Bureau Chief for Unified Media International.

Not one to shy away from nepotism, Kira used Robert's position to ascend the journalistic ladder, accepting posts in Madrid, Paris, and Moscow.

It was the campaign coverage of Vice President Hernandez, which brought her to the US. Her superiors felt her age as well as her gender would win the candidate over and, perhaps, lead to more intimate interviews.

Qualifications which resulted in the pair establishing a professional relationship based on their mutual disdain of gender-based assignments. The tacit and invisible barrier between reporter and quarry was shattered the day Kira happened to overhear Hernández embroiled in a less than amenable cell-phone conversation.

That the reporter knew Spanish was a bonus, because she heard the fired-up Latina snap at recipient of the call, "Just try relegating me to fucking window dressing, old man. I'll make sure you never get another Hispanic vote again, and that this party won't be able to truck voters over the border."

Stefi — a nickname Kira had come up with on the campaign trail because Estefanía was too much of a mouthful — turned to see the journalist scribbling so fast, she expected the woman's notepad to combust.

Their eyes locked, and Kira paused, her smirk informing Stefi, the latter's comments were better than gold.

"Look, I'll call you back," Stefi hung up.

Running a hand through the onyx-colored strands of her hair, she entreated, "Is there any way you can ignore what you just heard?"

"Surely you jest?"

"I don't, and don't call me Shirley?" Stefi joked, half-heartedly.

"That only works for Leslie Neilson."

"So what's it going to cost me? And don't say my soul, because you're too late for that. It was sold years ago."

"Okay, how about an exclusive interview, and a drink?"

"How about the drink first, then we'll see how I feel."

The two ended up downing a bottle of high grade whiskey and forgetting about the interview.

So began a beautiful friendship, at least, at times.

For the most part, it was Kira trying to get Stefi to verify some story, not even the VP was able to confirm… on record.

As the briefing concluded, a question from the back of the room snagged Kira's attention. These journalists were ignored because they were seen as unfavorable toward Hyden, and Foster left them wallowing in self-loathing for their error in judgment.

"Hey, Bill, Michael Grear, Conservative CounterCulture, is there any truth to the rumor, Hyden has moved a substantial number of troops into Przemyśl, near the Polish border with Ukraine?"

As a body, the crowd paused. All eyes focused on Foster

who stood by the exit, frozen not only by the unexpected question, but also by the overwhelming silence it elicited.

Another voice, from one of the White House's friendlies, interjected, "Is that true, Bill?"

His hand on the doorknob, the Press Secretary faced the crowd looking like a wounded antelope waiting for a pack of hyenas to tear him apart.

Clearing the knot in his throat, Foster tried to instill a note of confidence into his response, "Michael, while that is a question you should direct to the DOD, rest assured, any troop movement is part of a NATO exercise and bears no correlation to events unfolding in—"

At that precise moment, and to a person, every cell phone erupted in a cacophony of annoying ringtones.

Kira glanced at her screen to see houses ablaze, accompanied by the headline: **RUSSIAN MISSILES SLAM INTO PEACEFUL VILLAGE ON POLISH BORDER, DEATHS MOUNTING.**

The room exploded with questions clamoring for details, but Kira did not hang around for the standard government BS. Contrary to Foster's habitual evasiveness, it was obvious, he was as much in the dark as they were.

Reaching her car, Kira accessed the contact list on her phone. *If anyone had a credible answer, it would be him,* she thought. If *he still has his personal phone.*

Soundlessly, her EV pulled away from the White House gate before she pressed the green icon, wanting to ensure her call was not intercepted by the NSA… *accidentally.*

Hearing it ring twice, before being sent to voicemail was encouragement enough for Kira to spend the next hour redialing the number.

Lieutenant Colonel Leonid Ilyich Gusev was named for the man his father saw as the hero of the old Soviet Union, Leonid Brezhnev. The elder Gusev raised his son to stand firm against his political rivals, even if they happened to be American presidents.

There was one opposing force, who left him in her wake time and again. The same woman, currently blowing up his phone, no matter how many times he tried to dismiss the call.

Exasperated, he stormed into his office, inadvertently answering the call before his door slammed shut.

It was long enough for Kira to hear a frantic Russian voice yelling in the background, "...then find out from where the hell it *did* launch."

In an angry, haggard voice, Gusev barked into the phone, "Look, Kira, I don't have time for cordial chitchat right now, especially with you. So, if you—"

"Don't you dare hang up on me, Leo."

Her use of his nickname made him grimace. Kira Monroe was the only one at liberty to address him as such.

Even though his position in the Russian Ministry of Defence was Second Deputy Minister of Defence of the Russian Federation — Responsible for Organizing Material-Technical Support for the Armed Forces or… as he told Kira, frequently… a glorified Quartermaster, his rank granted him a modicum for respect.

Until the day his superiors discovered he had been sleeping with an American journalist.

It cost him a star from his shoulder, despite being unable to link him directly to specific leaks.

Still, lovers talk, and he found himself an unwitting unnamed source in one of her stories.

"Like I said, Kira, I don't have time for a gossip."

"Just answer one question. Are your generals drunk?"

"No, but after what we've discovered, I bet they wish they were."

There was a pause in the conversation.

"Come on, Leo. You know you can trust me."

"Da, to put me in an early grave."

With a heavy sigh, he admitted, thinking if a foreign press reported the denial it might be more believable, "The missiles were not ours."

"So I gathered. Any idea whose they were?"

"Not a single one. Somebody with deep pockets. The Ukrainians, maybe, hoping to drag willing Poles into the conflict, along with all of NATO. The Syrian Kurds, perhaps. God knows they have enough of our weapons."

"Nah," Kira disagreed. "Only if Turkey was attacked. Even then, NATO would turn a blind eye as usual."

"You are correct. That makes as much sense as thinking the last of the Romanovs planned it in hopes of regaining the Tsar's throne."

"This is more than saber-rattling. How will Russia react?" Kira's question was colored by genuine concern.

"What else can we do but deny responsibility."

Once again silence filled the line.

Unexpectedly, Leo asked, "Are you still in the business of quoting anonymous sources?"

"Come on, Leo, nobody will buy that, even if it is the truth. I have to tie somebody's name to the denial."

"Unless you want to write my obituary as well, the answer is no. I can assure you, no one in Moscow will query the validity of the story."

"Fine," Kira capitulated. "But, if I find out you're playing games with me, Leo, I'll personally lead the first Polish battalion through Belarus and into Russia."

Leonid sniggered. "You know I love a woman in uniform," as she disconnected the call.

CHAPTER FIVE

While the bulk of the newsreaders, and the communications departments of both parties, scrambled to throw in their two cents' worth on the missile attack across various media outlets, Kira had already published her byline.

Crediting unnamed sources within the Russian government, Kira's story boiled down to:

The Kremlin condemns the unprovoked attack on Polish sovereignty. Measures will be enacted by military and civilian law enforcement to ensure those responsible are brought to justice with all haste.

(Meaning executions or government funded vacations to Siberia.)

Moscow, as always, respects Polish independence (a blatant lie) *and will continue to stand in solidarity with the government in Warsaw in the war against terrorism, and offers any assistance they may need to recover and rebuild after this senseless attack.*

The response from the Russians and the media was instantaneous, although at one hundred and eighty degrees from each other.

While the Russian Minister of Foreign Affairs, Fyodor Mikhaylov, rushed around Europe declaring his country's innocence to any news organization prepared to listen, he also took pains to reassure his fellow NATO members, the attack was *not* a preemptive strike.

Mikhaylov praised the courage of the American journalist in reporting the truth, and not basing her story on spurious propaganda. He even went as far as to demand she receive the coveted American prize for journalism.

Polish media, on the other hand, posted the names and faces of the dead and missing nonstop, on television and in print.

Politicians from the Polish extremist parties appealed to NATO to enforce Article Five, and punish the Russians to the fullest military extent.

When Russia and China vetoed a resolution in the United Nations Security Council, condemning the *alleged* Russian attack, the Polish delegation walked out en masse and joined a pro-Poland rally in front of the building.

Inevitably, heads of state across the continent took sides. The western countries followed in line behind Poland, awaiting NATO's decision, while the Collective Security Treaty states, six former Soviet-era authoritarian countries which bordered Russia, martialed their armies for impromptu military exercises in their western territories.

In America, the right wanted the head of the Russian President Kirill Golubev to be served up on a silver platter to the Polish President, Bazyli Wojcik, in a gesture of conciliation for Russia's aggression.

The hardliners tried, desperately, to draw parallels between Russia's *unprovoked* rocket attack, and the Soviet Union's treatment of Poland during World War Two, comparing Golubev with Josef Stalin.

Their demands to send money, weapons and troops to

the Polish frontier, echoed along the halls of Congress and in front of the television cameras.

At the other end of the political spectrum, the left seized the opportunity to swing the spotlight away from their beleaguered occupant in the White House.

They appeared on every party-friendly talk show, deriding the right for denying due process for all participants to play out on the world stage, and of being war hawks, seeking any reason for the right's donors to profit from the pending war.

Simultaneously, they turned a blind eye to the fact, their own donors in Silicon Valley were about to reap huge rewards for the sales of military software and computer guidance systems to the same opponents.

Profiteering was of secondary concern to any of the commentators. Instructed by their producers — who were, in turn, ordered by their respective network bosses — to steer clear of any questions concerning Hyden's stance on the issue… which he took care of himself… the primary objective was to provide cover for the President.

Meanwhile, Hyden was busy on the campaign trail, discreetly drumming up support for the Poles.

As was the norm in Washington, subcommittees, chaired by members of the party in power and undermined by the opposition party, were convened immediately.

Television reported the circus from the opening gavel.

The Joint Chiefs of Staff were subpoenaed before these same dog and pony committees to determine America's reaction.

All responded in kind. "A measured retaliation, *if* the Russians are found to have committed a heinous act of war."

The NSA and CIA chiefs were summoned to the floor to explain why the Intelligence Services had failed to uncover the plot against a close American ally.

Answers were inconclusive, scarcely accomplishing anything more than one-upmanship between the political parties for the constituents.

Not all proceedings ended in the same useless political flag waving. One, in particular, deteriorated, meteorically, into chaos.

The full weight of the capital city felt as though it had fallen on the young journalist who broke the story originally, absolving Russia of its guilt. Both parties spent the better part of two days grilling her, in an attempt to compel her to change her tune.

At the hearing table for the Senate Foreign Relations Committee, Kira faced the up and coming star of the Republican Party, a certain Senator Frazier Tomlinson.

The Kentucky businessman's father had struck a bargain with the state's then governor, allowing Tomlinson junior to fill his seat some sixteen years earlier, following the death of his predecessor.

A survivor of two re-election campaigns... mostly running unopposed... he viewed today as the perfect time to sharpen his teeth on this woman's bones. To prove his nationalistic views — which, he was sure, would propel him to the forefront of the pack of Republicans running to unseat Hyden.

Settling back in his chair, Tomlinson asked casually, "Miss Monroe..." condescension thick in his tone, "...is it true your great grandfather was the famed journalist, Ted Monroe?"

The question caught Kira off guard for a moment, as she tried to figure out how this related to why they were here.

"Yes, Senator, but I fail—"

"Is it true, he was considered a Communist sympathizer?" he paused to push the power button on a remote, activating a monitor, displaying a number of yellowed newspaper clippings. "That, in the thirties, he was involved in a proposal to establish an exchange program…"

Tomlinson spoke with slow deliberation, "with Russian schools and, in the fifties, he challenged the notion of Communist infiltration in the US government?"

"Yes, your last two points are true, and a matter of historical record, which any five-year old with a search engine can find but, I assure you, my great grandfather was anything but a Communist. He was a dedicated journalist—"

"Who bent over backwards to support the Russians.

"Hardly, Senator. In fact, his philosophy was anti-Communist but, domestically—"

"Going as far as to criticize America's support of our allies in Greece in 1947, while they fought to repel the Communist threat backed by Russia—"

"He protested our country's excessive interference in that civil war—"

Tomlinson ignored Kira. "Since you brought up the word *domestically*," he emphasized sarcastically, "correct me if I'm wrong, but did he not go out of his way to oppose the policies of the Republican Party?

"Furthermore, I believe your father, Robert Monroe, also published a number of reports criticizing American policies in the Middle East and Afghanistan?

"Not exactly outstanding Americans from whom to craft your political views, missy."

"To reiterate, Senator, I fail to see the connection between—"

"I am sorry, Miss Monroe, my time has expired. I defer to my colleague from New York."

"If you would permit me to answer."

The Democratic Senator from New York had no stomach to challenge the Committee Chairman, and did not want to look weak in front of the media and his constituents on the subject of the Russians, especially since his seat was up for re-election in the next cycle.

He decided to play safe and repeat the same question his fellow party members had been asking for the past two days.

"Miss Monroe, if you want this committee to believe your assertion that the Russians should not be held responsible for this attack on Polish civilians, are you willing to divulge the names of your sources so we too can judge them credible?"

"As I've repeated until I'm blue in the face, Senator, doing so will endanger the safety of my sources."

"Miss Monroe," the man prodded, in what he hoped was a persuasive tone, "if the Russians are as innocent as you alleged, I doubt they would *kill the messenger*, per se. In fact, if we learned from where your source is in the hierarchy, it should bolster their case."

"Again, Senator, I respectfully decline the request from you and the committee."

The farce continued for the remainder of the session.

Before Tomlinson gaveled the end of the day, he felt it vitally important to put a stamp on the closing proceedings by lecturing the young woman, "Miss Monroe, I am disappointed by your attitude towards this committee and your refusal to answer our questions."

"Maybe if you had asked a single question, I could answer—"

As seemed to be his habit, he talked over Kira, "I have no doubt your great, grandfather and father are ashamed of your blatant disregard for national security. I can only pray to the Good Lord, you consider the consequences your lies may have caused the poor Poles."

"*Lies?*" Kira snapped back, the gavel falling before she could protest any further.

Preparing to launch into a tirade as the crowded room emptied, Kira felt hands hook her arms.

Two Capitol police officers stood behind her.

The older one said, "Miss, you are done for the day. Please come with us or you can have your lawyer bail you out from Metro."

Incensed, Kira gathered up her folders and notes from the table, determined to leave under her own volition.

Then her cell phone trilled.

A short message flashed on her phone, "I need to see you somewhere secure."

Without a second's thought, Kira Monroe threw a fit worthy of an academy award.

She tossed her papers about the committee room, none of which were of any importance, since she was not allowed to use them, jumped on the table, a feat in itself considering she was wearing heels, and grabbed the microphone.

Stomping on the polished surface, she protested at the top of her lungs, "These proceedings are unconstitutional. It is nothing but a witch trial against my family. Persecution! No justice! No peace! Attica! Attica!"

Along with any other political rhetoric which came to mind.

The guards grabbed Kira by her legs and pulled them out from under her, causing her to topple with a bang onto the table.

Restrained against the table, in a not so subtle fashion, Kira's arms were yanked behind her, handcuffs snapped around her wrists, and she was hauled out of the room.

Not before she yelled, "Soylent Green is made from humans."

To the delight of the photographers who, finally, had decent pictures to sell to the wires.

CHAPTER SIX

Kira had lost all sense of time since she entered the Correctional Treatment Facility, in South East DC.

No sooner had she been processed, her *one* call to her editor going unanswered, and gaged a risk to other detainees awaiting their turn, than she was frog-marched to a solitary holding cell as far from the rest of the facility's population as possible and, evidently, forgotten about.

Lying on the hard bench, she ruminated over why she had agreed to the text request so easily. The two had not actually spoken to each other recently.

Her stomach growled.

Kira shouted through locked door, "Hey, whoever's out there, I need food, and to be given the chance to make another call."

Knowing it was useless, she took off her shoe and used it to pound on the door. If this made her look crazier, so be it.

"I know my rights. You can't just starve me to death."

Eventually, a woman answered from the other side of the door, "Would a Big Mac shut you up?"

Kira recognized the voice.

"Only if you didn't forget the fries and a drink, and I'm not talking about a soda."

The door clanged open to reveal the Vice President in the corridor, a fast food bag in tow.

"They won't allow sodas in here, they're afraid you'd figure out how to use it to dissolve the mortar."

"How about I just use your head, Hernández."

"Now, now, you're already in enough trouble—"

"Yeah, thanks to you," Kira retorted.

"—so perhaps it's not a good idea to threaten the Vice President of the United States."

"Tell me, Madame Vice President, what was so important, I needed to come across as a January Sixth lunatic?"

Estefanía Hernández joined Kira on the bench and handed over the prison meal.

"You did a decent job of that. Consider yourself lucky, you only ended up here instead of the psych ward at St Elizabeth's, especially after tossing out an obscure Charlton Heston quote, incorrectly I might add." Stefi laughed.

"Oh, and I'd avoid TV cameras if I were you. You've been all over cable all day, and I'm pretty you're a couple of memes, too. Though I try to stay away from social media, so I'm not sure."

"Liar," Kira charged. "You forget I'm the one who discovered your secret account… *Gwendolyn*."

"Whatever," the VP shot back. "How long have we been friends?"

Kira realized this cryptic question was about to lead to why they were perpetrating this preposterous charade.

"Since the night in the back of your campaign bus when you got me drunk and had your way with me."

Stefi rolled her eyes. "First, you only wish and, for the millionth time, that never happened. It was just some bizarre alcohol-fueled fantasy."

"Sure, sure." Kira feigned a forlorn sniffle. "Typical politician, use the bright-eyed young journalist and toss…"

"Enough, Kira," Stefi cut her off, her expression no longer friendly. "I don't have long before my security detail is going to notice, I'm missing from my place."

"Okay, talk. What's going on?"

"Don't stop your investigation."

"You dragged me down here for that?"

"This is deeper than misdirected missiles."

"How deep?"

"My source at the NSA…"

"Wait, you have sources? Can I use them?

Ignoring the question, Stefi went on, "They were listening to the chatter going on in Belarus, when lo and behold, a corn-fed American voice broke in. It was just for a second, but there should not have been any Americans on that frequency."

"A ham radio operator?"

"Maybe, but why would an operator use the word, *Gunny*?"

"Have they determined where the missiles originated?"

"Somewhere along the Poland-Belarus border."

"That doesn't help much."

"No but it's given Hyden a reason to move F-35 Raptors to forward bases in Poland and *non-lethal*…"

"Meaning supposed non first-strike weapons?"

"Exactly, but the Ukrainians are in the process of receiving another ten billion dollars' worth of surface to air and anti-tank missiles, and the same supplies, in varying degrees, are being sent to countries from Finland to Turkey."

"Welcome back to the Cold War." Kira attempted to make light of the situation, to no avail.

"Except we are a few steps too close for the Russians' comfort, and most of the old Warsaw Pact has an axe to grind with Moscow. According to Intelligence, Golubev and the oligarchs have vacated Moscow for somewhere further east, but no one knows where.

"Then there is the training exercise, within fifty miles of the Belarus border, with the Poles, Germans and, of course, us, all at the behest of the Warsaw government."

"So, an accident waiting to happen?"

"More like a powder keg waiting for a match."

With that, the VP rose and knocked on the door, which swung open instantly.

Turning to look back at Kira, Stefi pleaded, "If you really do have an ear of somebody high up in the Russian Military, you need to convince them to draw down."

Kira rose and gathered her stuff to follow her friend out, but the female officer beside Stefi held her hand up, preventing the journalist from leaving the cell.

"Hey, Stefi, what gives?"

"You're still under arrest for your outburst in the Capitol Building."

"Which you forced me into. Besides, I can't do anything here."

"And I'm only the VP. I don't have Presidential Pardon Power. On the bright side, I managed to pull some strings and have your charges dropped from Domestic Terrorism to Destruction of Public Property. Seems you did quite a number on the hearing table.

"I'll see you are released on your own recognizance in the morning. Later, and keep in touch."

Before Kira could respond the door slammed shut on her.

She yelled, "Just wait 'til you read my scathing op-ed on Vice Presidential abuse of power when this is over."

True to the VP's promise, Kira was brought before the judge on the dot of nine the next morning.

Finally, Fortune had decided to smile upon the young journalist whose body ached from falling asleep upright on the bench.

To her surprise, Walter, her curmudgeon editor, felt disposed to send the company's lawyer to plead her case. She was sure Harry Cartwright's fees would be deducted from her next couple of pay-checks.

The lawyer advised, in hushed but no uncertain terms, "Keep your mouth shut and let me do my job."

Harry had no chance to flash his legal prowess.

The moment Judge Randolph Jaspers took his seat, he began his dressing down of the defendant.

"Mr. Cartwright, whatever legal doctrine or excuse you may think you have to justify your client's poor choices, I have neither the patience nor desire to listen.

"As for you, Miss Monroe, along with the rest of your generation, I have no time for your antics, so do not attempt to repeat your performance in my courtroom."

For the better part of twenty minutes, the judge expressed his displeasure of Kira Monroe, exacerbated because he had received a call from the West Wing of the White House, instructing… no dictating… what his decision in this case would be.

Running out of breath and red in the face, the man on the bench concluded, "…and if it was up to me, I would throw the book at you, Miss Monroe, for your insensitive behavior in the People's House, but the Senate's Sergeant at Arms has submitted a written affidavit stating that if you provide reimbursement for the damage caused to the historic table, it will be sufficient retribution."

Kira leaned close to Harry. "Damage? The cops slammed me on the tab—"

Harry snapped, "Shut it."

The judge smacked the gavel in warning. "Shut it **both** of you.

"If I was you, missy…"

Kira hated being called that.

"…I would write a letter of apology to him and Senator Tomlinson, thanking them for their leniency."

Seeing the disingenuous look on the woman's face, he amended his opinion, choosing to ramp it up.

"No, on second thoughts, the terms of your restitution are as follows. A fine of two-thousand dollars for the table repair, and a letter of apology to each of the Senate committee members, acknowledging your misdeeds and pleading for absolution."

"W-What?" the journalist stammered. "You cannot be serious, your honor. I think that is unconstitutional or, at the very least, cruel and inhumane."

The judge banged his gavel again, harder than before. "One more outburst, miss, and I will have you jailed for contempt."

Harry tried to diffuse the situation. "I am sorry, your honor—"

"As you should be, Mr. Cartwright," Jaspers barked. "If your client has a problem with my sentence, take it up with the Supreme Court."

"That won't be necessary, your honor. It's more than fair under the circumstances."

From the corner of his eye, Harry saw his client readying to open her mouth to express her opinion on what he surmised to be the validity of the American Justice System. As though squashing a bug, he stepped firmly on her foot.

"Get her out of my court, Mr. Cartwright," Jaspers ordered, "before I toss you both in jail."

Waiting for his driver outside the courthouse, Harry lit a cigarette. Flicking his designer lighter closed and tucking it in his pocket, he quipped, "Well, that went well if I do say so myself."

"Compared with what? A public flogging?" Kira sniped.

Exhaling a lungful of smoke, he leveled a gaze at his client. "You're standing on the sidewalk, aren't you?"

"Yeah, but the evil teacher is making me write twenty-five times, *I'm sorry for having an opinion.*"

"Bah, don't worry about that. We can appeal the ruling to the point, he's retired before you ever but pen to paper."

A Nautic Blue Mercedes-Maybach S-Class rolled to a halt. The uniformed driver, trained to stop with meticulous care, hopped out to hold the rear door open for the lawyer, tipping his hat deferentially.

Without acknowledging the man, Harry climbed in.

The driver paused to make sure the woman was not joining his employer. When she did not move, he closed the door with a soft click, and returned to his seat.

Harry wound down the window, bidding Kira goodbye with a parting shot, "If needs be, I'm happy to represent you before the justices…" the car started to pull away, "…and I'll only charge you the company rate of $350 an hour."

CHAPTER SEVEN

Scouring everything she could about the missile attack on the village of Włodawa in Poland, Kira came across an odd story from Minsk.

An American Marine, reported AWOL from his platoon, took his own life after murdering a local citizen. Allegedly, drugs and weapons were discovered in the hotel room.

Local authorities have determined the American was the ring-leader of a gang, smuggling contraband.

The body is awaiting extradition to his home of Aplington, Iowa, US.

Jumping up from her desk, Kira burst into Walter's office, waving the report.

"How may I be of service, Miss Monroe? Maybe, I can start by teaching you how to knock on a door?"

"Takes too much time, Walter."

"That's Mister—" Walter started and then gave up on the notion of schooling this woman in the finer points of etiquette. "What do you want?"

"A plane ticket to Iowa."

"What the hell is in Iowa besides too many white Republican voters?"

Kira blinked in disbelief at this statement. "Christ, Walter, that's racist even for you."

He waved a dismissive hand at her. "Why do you need to go to Iowa? The caucus isn't gonna be held there for a couple of months."

Dropping the sheet of paper on his desk, Kira explained, "I want to talk to his family before anybody else does."

"Again, I ask why?"

"What are the odds a twenty-something-year-old from Iowa is an international arms dealer, let alone having the wherewithal to make it all the way to Belarus while on the run from the US military?"

"Go. Get out of what little hair I have left."

True to Walter's nature, the man went out of his way to ensure his reporter was booked on the most inconvenient flight he could find. In addition to being the cheapest airline with service to Des Moines, Iowa, taking off from Reagan National at seven in the morning, it also flew past the city entirely, requiring a two hour layover in Denver.

It was close to five in the afternoon by the time Kira's, equally cut-rate, rental car rolled up in front of the home of Corporal John Wayne Davis.

There were no other reporters around. Somewhat confused, Kira looked at her watch to make sure she had not lost days in her convoluted journey to get here.

Relieved there had not been a time warp, she frowned, perplexed at being, seemingly, the only American, nay international journalist who was perturbed by the coincidence of Davis's supposed suicide.

Kira climbed the cement steps from the curb to the path

leading to the front door, registering that every house on the block mirrored the same well-manicured lawn as the Davis's yard.

Welcome to Middle America, she mocked internally. *Make sure to take off your shoes before using our sidewalks.*

She trudged up the last four steps to the porch which shaded the facade of the early twentieth-century bungalow. A closer look at the framing of the house revealed its need for a fresh coat of paint.

I guess everything in life can be deceptive.

Not finding a bell… *how quaint…* Kira knocked on the door. She stood there for a minute or so before knocking once again, this time calling out, "Mrs. Davis? It's Kira Monroe, we spoke on the phone last night."

No response.

Looking around her, Kira jiggled the doorknob, startled to discover it was unlocked, the door popping open.

Pushing the door wider, Kira called out again, "Mrs. Davis?"

The stench of natural gas seared her nostrils and made her eyes water. Pulling a handkerchief from her pocket — something her grandmother had insisted she carry, now a habit she could not shake — Kira raced to the kitchen.

The oven door was open, gas hissing from it and the four rings on the stove top.

Shutting everything off, she opened the back door to air out the house.

Choking on the noxious, rotten egg fumes, Kira searched the one story house for the owner. She did not have to hunt far, the woman's bedroom was across the hall from the kitchen.

Mrs. Davis was lying on her bed. Next to her, atop a small wooden cabinet, an open prescription bottle tipped on its side, a handful of pills spilling onto the polished surface.

Although registering that the bottle contained sleeping pills, Kira was more concerned about Mrs. Davis, shaking her violently, and shouting, "Wake up. We need to get out of here."

Noticing the blue-ish tinge of the woman's lips, Kira grabbed her under the arms, and hauled her outside.

While she had taken CPR classes when a kid, Kira could not recall the steps, and called the emergency services to report a gas leak and Mrs. Davis's condition.

It took about ten minutes for the gas company and the EMT's to arrive. The gas company did a cursory check of the house to clear themselves of culpability for the leak, ascertaining the woman had turned the gas on deliberately.

The rescue squad attempted to resuscitate Mrs. Davis as they prepped her for transport to the nearest hospital in Waterloo.

One of the EMTs pushed Kira aside. "Look, miss, if we have any chance to save Charity here, you're gonna have to stay out of our way."

"Charity? You know her?" Kira did the one thing every tech detests, asking, "Can I ride along?"

He shot her an annoyed look. "I know you're not related, so, that would be no," and slammed the ambulance door on the journalist.

The trip to Waterloo was forty miles. Even at the speed the ambulance was traveling, it was going to take nearly half an hour to get there.

They passed the sheriff's car on the way out of town. Lights flashing and the siren blaring its warning to clear the way, Hank, the driver, figured Sheriff Harkin was on his way to Mrs. Davis's place.

The EMT in the back with Charity Davis was trying valiantly to save the woman. About halfway there, a call came over the radio. The tech did not listen to the conversation between the driver and dispatch.

"Hey, Barry, get this," Hank called over his shoulder after returning the radio's mic to its holder. "Jen just said the hospital found a DNR in Charity's hospital records. Didn't we resuscitate her a couple of months ago when she had her heart attack?"

Hearing his patient had a Do Not Resuscitate order on file, Barry ceased CPR, just when her nearest response to a breath occurred, the air in her lungs escaping in a sighed huff.

Barry swung his gaze to the front of the ambulance, his eyes meeting Hank's in the mirror.

"That can't be right. Have them check again."

"Jen already said they verified it. According to the records, it was added before she was discharged last time. Funny thing is, no one remembered her doing it, but I guess she was just tired of it all."

"Did Harkin mention to Jen whether Miss Charity left a suicide note?" Barry frowned, studying Charity. He had known the woman his whole life. She had been his grade school teacher and his Sunday school teacher.

"Jen didn't say one way or the other."

Barry noted the almost serene expression on the elderly woman's face. Softly, he said, "I'll miss you, Miss Charity."

CHAPTER EIGHT

Kira caught up with the ambulance at the hospital, as the EMT's were about to return to the station. Kira had other ideas.

Coming to a halt in front of the vehicle, something her dad had taught her when handling uncooperative witnesses, she climbed out of the rental and leaned against the driver's side fender.

Wanting to get back to the meal waiting for him, Hank pressed the horn. Others in the parking lot glanced their way at the commotion, but Kira refused to move.

"I have a couple of questions for that one." She pointed at Barry. "And I don't plan on budging until he agrees."

Hank looked at his partner, and shrugged. "You heard her, out."

"What the hell, man? You're going to leave me with some crazy woman?"

"Who knows, you might get lucky. 'Sides, I'm starving and my steak is probably getting stone cold while we stand here arguing. So, out."

Climbing down, Barry groused, "I hope you choke on it, and I'm not there to save you."

"I'll risk it." Switching his attention to the woman, he shouted, "He's all yours. Now, get out of the way."

Kira tipped a cynical salute to the driver, and moved her car. Stopping in front of Barry, she rolled down the window.

"I'll drive you back, so get in."

"If I don't?"

"I'll park this piece of shit on your foot until you agree."

Shaking his head in disbelief, somehow sure she was serious, he got into the passenger seat.

"Can I at least ask who's abducting me?" Barry asked, only half joking.

She grinned cheerfully. "Kira Monroe, Unified Media International." Shifting the car into drive, she started, "So, tell me, did you know John Wayne Davis?"

"JW," Barry replied.

"Excuse me?"

"JW, that's what we called him. He hated being called John Wayne. His dad was a huge fan of Westerns, which is how he got his name. He spent most of high school fighting guys because of it. Stupid, huh? I guess it didn't help that JW was, how do the proper folks say it, *special*."

"Special?" Kira repeated, knowing what he meant, but not prepared to take anything for granted.

"Yeah, you know, not the sharpest knife in the drawer. Most guessed it was because of the drugs his mom did when she was carrying him; but that's above my medical training."

"Wait, Charity Davis was into drugs when she was pregnant with JW? At her age?"

"Huh? Miss Charity was his grandmother."

Kira's nose wrinkled in confusion. "Where are his parents?"

"Dead, both of them. Killed in a drug shoot-out in Chicago. That was where JW was born."

Barry dragged his gaze from the view beyond the windshield, to the driver. "I'm guessing by the look on your face, you didn't bother to do your research before you came all this way."

"I-I talked to Charity—"

"Mrs. Davis to you. You don't have the right to call her by her first name."

"Mrs. Davis did not say anything about being his grandmother when I talked to her on the phone last night."

"Wait, you talked to her last night? What time?"

"I don't know, maybe seven or so, your time."

"After which she turned her stove on and killed herself. What the fuck did you say to her?"

"Hey, whoa, I swear I didn't say anything to upset her," Kira refuted, hotly. "Don't make this my fault. All I did was ask whether I could come visit with her. I had questions about her son's, I mean, grandson's death."

"It couldn't wait until she got the ashes back? Because of his *situation*, the Government wouldn't even cover the cost of shipping a casket home with his remains, so they cremated him. She was told they would come back parcel post. Can you believe that?"

His eyes back on the road, he muttered, "Like hell he was a deserter."

"About him being AWOL. Is that in his nature?"

Barry didn't reply immediately, and the silence stretched out between them.

Finally. "The Marines were everything to him. He used to send Miss Charity pictures of wherever his duty stations took him. He told her it gave him a feeling of belonging. For him to be anywhere except where he was supposed to be, makes no sense."

"The charges of dealing drugs and weapons?"

"After his parents were murdered, his grandmother did everything she could to keep him on the straight and narrow. Besides, he didn't have it in him to be an international criminal mastermind like the government is alleging. We were amazed they took him in the first place, and would a drug dealer join the strictest branch, or any branch for that matter, of the military?"

Kira glanced at Barry. He was physically shaken, but it was imperative she extract as much information as possible before he clammed up.

"Was Mrs. Davis the type to become so overwhelmed, her only escape was to kill herself?"

"Are you kidding? She was a, excuse the expression, a Churchie. Suicide was a sin, she said could never be forgiven. The woman had already buried her son and daughter-in-law, leaving her to raise their child on her own. She had more strength in her heart than anyone I knew."

"In that case, am I to assume, she would be unlikely to overdose, deliberately?" Kira ventured, bracing herself for another tongue lashing.

"Not a chance. Wait… overdose?" Barry stared at Kira, who told him about the pill bottle.

"No, no way," Barry said emphatically. "Miss Charity hated pills and, to my knowledge, never required any help sleeping, even after she got sick. Used to say the only blessing was she never had any problem getting a good night's sleep."

Kira's mental note was becoming an essay.

"Do you know if they found a suicide note?" she asked.

"You would know better than me," he snapped. "You were the first one in the house. Did you see one?"

"N-No," Kira stammered, "but I wasn't looking for one at the time."

Barry sighed, "No idea. Jen didn't say. I guess you're

gonna have to ask the sheriff if he found one. Knowing him, its unlikely he'll even check for one, satisfied everything is neatly tied up already."

They were approaching the fire station. Kira was running out of time to get any more details.

"Barry, is there anything else you can think of that would throw light on Mrs. Davis's death?"

Shaking his head, Barry broke down.

To see a man express his feelings took Kira by surprise. She doubted she would see anything like that in DC.

Just a different lifestyle out here in the sticks, I guess.

Dropping Barry off, she thanked him for everything, but he walked away without a word in response.

Watching him disappear into the building, Kira let their conversation roll around her head, then pointed the car at the Butler County Sheriff's office.

Sheriff Elroy Harkin was busy filling out the incident report on Charity Davis when a young, attractive woman with a sour disposition entered his office.

"Sheriff Harkin?"

"That's what it says on the door you barged through. How may I be of assistance, Miss…?"

"Monroe. Kira Monroe, Unified Media International."

"What brings a big city… I'm assuming you're from some-where east—"

"Yes, I'm from our Washington, DC bureau."

"…DC reporter to our corner of Iowa? You're a bit early for caucus commentary but, if you really need a quote, Bob the Dog has my vote."

"Hardly, Sheriff. I'm here about Mrs. Davis's suicide. Do

you not find it too much of a coincidence that her beloved grandson commits suicide and then she follows suit?"

"I'd remind you to be respectful, missy."

Kira ground her teeth at being called missy again.

"As to the question of whether, the good Mrs. Davis committed suicide, I have no reason to believe otherwise. The gas was on, there was an almost empty bottle of pills next to her bed, and no forced entry, besides your intrusion, which reminds me, I'm gonna need a set of prints to match the ones I found on the front doorknob.

"As for the mental state of my recently departed life-long friend, in addition to losing her kin, she also was informed by Doc Blevins she had terminal female cancer."

"Female cancer?"

"Yeah, ya know, down there," Harkin said, pointing with no modicum of decency at Kira's crotch. "So, yeah, I can see her beseeching the Good Lord to take her home."

"And that's that?"

"Pretty much, unless you have evidence to contradict my findings and, if you don't, I bid you a good afternoon."

Seeing she was not about to gain anything else from Harkin, Kira turned to leave. Reaching the door, Harkin reminded her, "Oh, and Miss Monroe, don't forget to leave your prints and a business card with my Deputy, *just* in case we need to talk again."

CHAPTER NINE

"Sir?" Margaret's voice intruded, as Hyden sat at his desk doing a crossword puzzle.

Tossing his pencil into a cupful of matching yellow, wooden mates, Hyden steeled himself before he responded. He hated upbraiding his faithful secretary for interrupting his quiet periods but, as ever, she had the worst timing.

Increasing his testy disposition, he had missed his afternoon snooze. *If Reagan could get away with it, why can't I?* was Hyden's mantra regarding naps. Besides, his current sleeping pattern was erratic at best. *Heavy is the burden of leadership.*

Collecting himself, Hyden pressed the *Reply* button.

"Yes, Margaret?"

"FBI Director Sullivan is here to see you."

Lost in his crossword, Hyden had neglected to keep an eye on the clock. A glance had told him his appointment was five minutes early. It was a trait he respected in Connors... that and being a yes man.

"Send him in. Oh, and Margaret, make sure we are not disturbed."

"Yes, sir."

Sullivan entered the Oval Office not looking like a confident man in charge of the principle investigative arm of the DOJ, nor the person he had, scant days ago, asked to replace that backstabbing snipe who currently occupied the West Wing of the White House.

In fact, in Hyden's opinion, the man looked as though he was about to expel whatever he had for lunch.

"Connor, sit, sit, my boy," Hyden said, extending his hand to the chair across the desk from him. "You don't look well."

Fingers on the phone, Hyden asked with as much saccharine concern as he could manage, "Should I call for the White House physician to give you a once over? Ya know, I can't have my right hand man succumbing to stomach flu now, can I?"

Sullivan declined the offer politely. "No, thank you, sir. I assure you I'm physically fit." Thinking...*and the last thing I want is for* that *quack to shoot me up with anything from his magic bag.*

"Have you given any more consideration to running as my VP? We both know neither the country, nor the Democratic Party, can afford to leave that divisive bitch on the ticket." Hyden resumed his seat, adding with a cheesy grin, "Like I said before, *you and I* would make the perfect team."

It was then, he noticed an open manila folder on the FBI Director's lap.

Flipping through a ream of papers, Sullivan pulled a single sheet from its depths, and replied, "I'll give you an answer, Mr. President, when you answer a question of mine. Why is some redneck sheriff from Iowa calling my office for assistance in handling a DC reporter's questions about the kid in Minsk who topped himself?" Sullivan slid the page across the desk.

It was a telephone transcript.

"What the hell's going on, Jay, because this smacks of a

government coverup and I don't intend to get stuck holding anyone else's baggage."

"Connor, my boy, calm down." Jamison rose from his chair and rounded the desk, ignoring the document.

He placed his hands on Sullivan's shoulders in a fatherly fashion. Without breaking character, Hyden smiled and lied to his potential running mate, "It's just some overzealous reporter, no doubt trying to make a name for themselves at the expense of someone else's misfortune. Whatever story they think is out there has nothing to do with our administration."

Perching on the edge of the desk, his demeanor relaxed, Hyden repeated, "Far more importantly, can I count on your support, Connor? Will you accept history's summons and run as my Vice President?"

"Under one condition, Jay." Sullivan heaved himself out of his chair. "If I find you are bullshitting me, on anything, I will see you burn in front of Congress. Trust me, I know where the bodies are buried."

"As you should, given you put most of them there yourself," the President reminded the Director of his culpability.

After an awkward moment of mutual political threats, Hyden, the consummate politician, thrust out his hand. "Let me be the first to welcome you aboard."

Half-expecting to spy a knife hidden in his running mate's other hand, Sullivan accepted Hyden's mealy handshake. It spoke of a man who had never done an honest day's work in his life, even if he *had* hoodwinked America into thinking otherwise.

"I'll have Margaret email you the campaign schedule. Make sure to clear your calendar for those dates. We are about to race across the country to close the distance between us and those damned Judases running against us for our party's nomination."

Kira was on the late night flight back to DC, via a two and a half hour layover at Chicago's O'Hare Airport, when she caught the news on the plane's onboard television.

...and in other news, President Jamison Hyden held a joint news conference this evening officially announcing his intention to run for re-election.

The video flashed to the Oval Office where Hyden was seated on the couch next to the FBI Director.

With the look of a man aged beyond his years, but refusing to acknowledge it, he spoke to America.

"My fellow citizens, it has been my heartfelt pleasure to serve you these many decades, especially the last four as your President. Some, even within the Democratic Party, have expressed their concern that my better days are over."

As though aware of his stance, he straightened up.

"I guarantee, my best is awaiting your vote. I pledge to serve every American, regardless of political persuasion, we are one under the banner of our great flag. To demonstrate my resolve to reach out to the younger generation..."

Hyden stepped to aside to allow Sullivan to stand front and center.

"...I am pleased to introduce my personal choice as the next Vice President, Connor Sullivan."

Kira nearly choked on her cup of coffee, well aware Stefi was planning to run for President of her own volition, and had set the date to make her announcement from the Capitol steps.

Hyden had beaten her to the punch. Worse, he had not offered any explanation as to why he was dropping her from the ticket, or mentioned her at all.

This left Stefi's campaign with the problem of shedding the image of her running as petty revenge on her part.

The two men on the screen continued to extoll each other's virtues, until Kira wanted to use one of the vomit bags in the seat pocket.

Once the men completed their platitudes, the screen returned to the commentator, who finished the segment with a jab at the current occupant of the position, "We reached out to Vice President Estefanía Hernández for a comment, but our calls went unanswered.

"We will bring you more information as they develop."

Kira switched off the monitor and jotted on her phone, *Call Stefi as soon as I land.*

CHAPTER TEN

Sitting at the departure gate, awaiting the final leg of her journey to DC, Kira dialed Stefi's private line.

The phone rang twice when the masculine voice of Stefi's boyfriend, Francisco, answered.

"Hey, Kira. I'm astonished it took you this long to call."

"Hello, Cisco. How is Stefi taking the news?"

"Well, we're at my place if that tells you anything."

"Yikes!"

"Tell you what, why don't you ask her yourself?" he offered, a smile in his voice.

The voice of an angry Latina spewing every obscenity, she could come up with grew louder, and Kira assumed Cisco was holding the phone away from his ear.

She sniggered inwardly, imagining Stefi's abuela washing out her granddaughter's mouth with soap and water at the number of times *puta* colored the conversation.

Cisco came back on, chuckling. "That is, if you can get a word in edgewise?"

"Okay, I'll take my chances."

With a grin, Kira could not see over the phone, Cisco said, "It's your funeral.

"Love of my life…" Kira heard Cisco call out tentatively. "…you have a phone call."

"If it's that puta madre Hyden, tell him he can go—"

"Hon, manners."

Hundreds of miles away, Stefi snatched the phone from her man, mouthing… *and you're a pendejo.*

"***What***?" Stefi snarled at Kira's avatar on the screen. "Consider yourself lucky, you're not from CNN, MSNBC, or Fox. I have no comment for any of those suck-ups."

"Cool," she heard the teasing note in Kira's voice. "Then you're willing to talk to Unified—"

"Absolutely not. I know anything I say to you about what's going on will come back to haunt me."

"Then I guess this is going to be a short conversation."

"Fuck you, too," Stefi snapped, knowing her friend was trying to cheer her up.

"Any idea how he managed to outmaneuver you?"

"No… and I hate to think I have a mole on my staff."

"But it's a possibility?"

"For the right money, anything is possible," Stefi lamented.

"Are you still going through with your announcement as scheduled?"

"Do I have a choice? I can't very well put off the Speaker of the House and House Minority Whip can I?"

Glaring at Cisco, Stefi added, "Besides, my lug of a boyfriend finally remembered to ask for leave that day, so I can't let him off the hook."

· · ·

At the departure gate, Kira, a broad grin on her face and wondering whether the pair remembered she was there, heard Cisco attempt to defend himself, "Love, I've already explained why. It's only been a couple of months since the promotion... I couldn't very well up and ask for time off so soon."

"To be by your fiancée's side while she announces the second biggest decision—" Stefi let slip.

"*Second?*" Kira yelled into the phone to interrupt the side conversation, as the import of Stefi's remark registered.

"Wait... *fiancée?*" Stunned momentarily speechless, Kira removed her phone from her ear and gawped at the screen — *engaged... who'd a thunk it?* — then tucked it back against her shell-like.

"—life."

"And I told you, I'll be right by your side," Kira heard Cisco placate, although his tone bordered on teasing. She shook her head at their banter.

"Okay, you two lovebirds, break it up, and finish talking to me."

"Don't forget to show up, mister, or I'll have the Secret Service drag you out of your office in cuffs."

Kira chuckled, glad her friend still managed to maintain her sense of humor.

"Rumor has it, you ruffled some feathers in Iowa." Now, not very subtly, it was Stefi's turn to fish, but hoping to trick information out of Kira was a waste of breath.

"Let's just say, I'm lucky I left the state before I got an extended tour of the Iowa State Penitentiary," was all Kira was prepared to divulge.

"You gonna make me wait to read your byline?"

"Along with the rest of America. One last question?"

"After getting dissed on my question, why should I answer yours?"

"Because I'm cute and you love me? And I know you'll eventually get tired of Cisco and want to marry me… especially since you already had your way—"

"Oh, for Christ's sake, just ask."

"Which camp was the Marine AWOL from?"

"Lejeune. Why?"

"Is that handsome brother of yours still stationed with the JAG's Corps in DC?"

"Again, why?"

"Okay, I'll take that as a yes. Thanks, hon. You're a doll."

"Kira Monroe, tell me—"

"Congratulations, by the way," Kira interrupted and cut the call before Stefi could finish her question.

Kira was unaware her abrupt disconnection had earned her a barrage of Spanish obscenities out-weighing those Stefi had hurled at Hyden; neither did she know her friend was unable to prevent an ecstatic grin at Kira's good wishes.

As soon as Kira hung up, a third party on the call disconnected. Inside a van, identifying itself as belonging to the District of Columbia Water and Sewer Authority, two men had spent the last two days following the Vice President discreetly, in order to listen in on her personal telephone calls.

Hernández's decision to spend the night at her lover's house instead of her residence at the Naval Observatory made their job easier, because the brownstone in Georgetown had none of the advanced electronics which normally made this type of exercise near impossible.

Picking up a two way radio, one of the two keyed the mic.

"This is Richardson."

"Go ahead."

"The subject received a call from Chicago requesting information about the deactivated asset."

Hutchinson hated this cloak and dagger bullshit. That stuff was better left to the spooks, but they were hard to trust as well.

"What was requested?" Hutchinson asked all the same.

"Point of origin," was the reply.

"Shit," was all Hutchinson thought to say, before tossing the radio aside and picking up his secure line to call in a long-held favor from the occupant in the Marine Barracks in Washington, DC.

Lieutenant Juan Hernández looked at his watch. Grumbling about being disturbed from the first decent night's sleep in a week, for the *second* time, made him less cordial than when he answered the first call from his sister.

He had justified answering that one because... *even if she is a pain in the ass, she is still the Vice President.*

His reward for answering was a cryptic, "Whatever you do, don't answer the next call."

Sure enough it came, from a number he knew well. He had made the mistake of dating her for a few months after his sister had won her place in history — something the latter was unaware of at the time.

Hitting the decline button, Hernández sent the call to voicemail.

Which displeased the caller who rang back immediately.

The second call earned, *Power Off.*

Thirty-seconds later, the shrill clanging of the landline he had forgotten he owned, shattered the quiet. He dragged himself out of bed to hunt it down. Unlike his cell phone, he knew this antiquated form of communication was not tied to an answering machine, meaning the insistent ringing would not stop on its own.

Finding it buried under a stack of files, he complained into the handset, "You were already on my *No Call* list, Miss Monroe, even before Stefi warned me you would ring. Don't make me add you to the FBI's National Stalkers List, as well."

"Come on, Juan, we both know there's no such thing."

"Be that as it may, whatever you want, forget it. I'm done playing your games. I was done a long time ago. You don't get to fuck with my head, or my heart, twice."

"Geez, Juan, that was a long time ago when I was young and stupid."

"From what I hear from Stefi, you're still stupid."

"Ouch… that hurt and was totally uncalled for. Besides, I didn't take you for a guy who holds grudges. Okay, so I messed up, but you weren't exactly a gentleman now, were you? How was I supposed to know you wanted to be serious? You spent more time ogling the fake boob brigade than giving me your undivided attention.

"Can't we move on and behave like adults? This is really important and you're the only person I can trust. Give me a hard time later, but for now, please just listen."

"One minute. Starting now."

Given Juan might well be timing her, Kira launched in. "The kid who committed suicide in Belarus, are you aware his grandmother just did the same?"

"Fifty-seconds. No and why should that matter to either of us?"

"Because it was out of her norm to consider such a thing, even under the circumstances."

"Forty-seconds."

"You're not helping!"

"Thirty-five."

"Grrr… and from what I just learned, the kid bled Marine blue and red, and did not have the mental capability to—"

"Thirty-seconds."

"Christ, Juan, whatever is behind this kid's death has nothing to do with him being a deserter. He's being framed for something bigger and, if I took a guess, it has something to do with the missile strike in Włodawa."

The countdown paused.

In fact, the line went silent. *Has Juan hung up on me?*

"Juan?" she said hesitantly.

"Okay, let's just say you have piqued my curiosity, what do you want me to do?"

"I need you to get me onto the base at Camp Lejeune."

"Hold up, woman, it's going to take more than just your gut-feeling to get you onto a military facility."

"What is it going to take to get you to help?"

"In case you've forgotten, I am a lawyer… so, facts. Then again, you always did have a tough time separating truth from fiction, is that a prerequisite for a reporter."

"Hey, enough already, don't question my integrity," Kira shot back, trying to mask her annoyance at Juan's belligerence and failing miserably. "What would qualify as evidence worthy of you getting off your ass and investigating."

"Well, since this is not a TV show, cause of death would help."

"I don't understand," Kira responded, caught off guard.

"Prove to me it was anything but a suicide, and then we can talk."

"But don't you have the autopsy file from Minsk?"

Juan laughed.

"Call me when you have something concrete. Until then, burn this number."

CHAPTER ELEVEN

Seven Days Later

Kira had been trying to reach Lieutenant Colonel Leonid Ilyich Gusev for several days. If her call *did* reach his office, his gatekeeper of a military attaché informed her, Gusev was either out or unavailable.

Even his personal cell went unanswered, leaving Kira no alternative but to flood his voicemail until she could no longer leave messages.

As much as she hated going over his head, he left her no choice.

Out of desperation… and admittedly, no small amount of spite… she placed a call to her newest fan, Russian Minister of Foreign Affairs, Fyodor Mikhaylov.

To her amazement, the minister was in and willing to talk to her.

"Ah, Miss Monroe, to what do I owe the pleasure of this call?"

"Minister Mikhaylov, thank you—"

"Miss Monroe, for the service you tried, valiantly, to provide for Mother Russia, please call me Fyodor."

The information Kira had garnered on the Foreign Minister, besides being a notorious flirt and drinker, described him as a no-nonsense moderate, a family man with a large brood, and the son of a former Communist Party Official who helped revert Leningrad to the glorious city of St. Petersburg.

Being the son of a Party member did not disadvantage Mikhaylov growing up. Most of the *Reformists* were rebranded Communists. This meant the young Mikhaylov was afforded an education at the finest private boarding school then university Russia had to offer.

Upon graduation, Mikhaylov used his father's name to be appointed to prized posts within the Russian Foreign Service.

"Only if you will call me Kira, Minister."

"Then Kira it is. How may this — how do you Americans say? — humble civil servant be of assistance?"

"Well, Min… I mean Fyodor, I am in search of the results of an autopsy which should have been done in Minsk."

"My dear Kira, I fear Belarus is an autonomous country beyond my realm of influence. Any information you might need would have to come from the government there."

"Please, Fyodor, I do not have time to chase my tail through Belarusian bureaucracy. We both know how closely the governments of Moscow and Minsk are aligned."

Kira heard Mikhaylov chuckle at the politically correct description of the Belarusian dictator's deference to all things Russian.

"We do enjoy a unique relationship. I'm sure I can use the proper channels to get you the information you need. If I may ask the name of the person in question?"

"John Wayne Davis."

There was no response, the line had fallen quieter than a graveyard.

The name was becoming a greater enigma with each response.

The silence stretched out.

Kira was on the verge of a banshee yell… simply to elicit a reaction… when Mihaylov spoke, "There is no need to bother anyone in Minsk about this individual. Have you considered approaching his former superiors at the Camp Lejeune Marine Base?"

"Fyodor, again, you and I know how we Americans pride ourselves on dragging our feet if it does not benefit us."

Her comment elicited another soft chuckle.

"This is what I know, my friend. Your fellow countryman died as a result of cranial damage sustained from the—"

"Wait, Fyodor, did you say cranial damage? I won't bother to ask why you happen to have a copy of an autopsy—"

"Which never occurred."

"Which never occurred? How did they rule his death a suicide without a post mortem? Does that not imply he was pushed from the balcony rather than jumped?"

"Not necessarily, my dear."

"Fyodor…"

"But yes, I agree it does look somewhat suspicious under the circumstances."

"And the toxicology report?"

"What toxicology report?"

"You're telling me, the police in Minsk did not think to check whether there were any drugs in his system when he died?"

"They assumed, given the amount of cocaine and meth-amphetamine found in the hotel room, along with the dead prostitute, there was no necessity."

"His remains?"

"Cremated and turned over to the American Ambassador in Minsk."

"Thank you for your invaluable help, Fyodor. I will not interfere with your duties any longer."

"Before you hang up, Kira, may I plead a favor in return?"

"I'm not sure how I can be of any help to you, Fyodor, but please, go ahead."

"Why was your government so determined to destroy this man's body, yet demanded it back?"

"I wish I could give you a suitable answer, Fyodor. When I have one, I promise to let you know."

"Perhaps, at that time, you will visit me in my beautiful home city of St. Petersburg and allow me to take you out to dinner as my way of saying thank you."

"With Mrs. Minister of Foreign Affairs, of course."

Kira sensed the smile in his response, "But, of course."

Two days later, while Kira was going through her notes, she turned on the Thursday night football game.

Stefi had paid big bucks, with the DNC's help, to make her announcement for President during the game's half-time show.

As the second quarter ended, and the commentators jostled back and forth about how both defenses were making this a slow game, the network broke to the steps of the Capitol Building. A scene repeated on the other major networks.

Vice President Estefanía Hernández stepped up to a lectern, almost obscured by the array of microphones.

Behind her, the two men from opposite parties, who owed a generous portion of their political success to her, as well as the man the VP had threatened to arrest if he failed to appear.

Kira watched as her friend drew a breath to gather the courage necessary to face the country and proclaim her intention to be their next President.

"Ladies and Gentlemen, permit me to introduce myself. I am Vice President Estefanía Hernández, and I stand before you tonight to announce—"

Suddenly, the network interrupted her, breaking in with the image of the Presidential podium against a backdrop of American flags, flanked by a member of each of the armed services, in full dress uniform.

Behind the camera, the Press Room was empty.

The screen stayed that way, frozen in time, for five minutes.

Successfully preempting his chief political rival, President Jamison Hyden entered stage left and took his place behind the podium, were there was but one microphone.

This guaranteed every American watching saw his expression, which read like the lone soul charged with a decision which would bring death to others in his name. Gathering himself, he addressed the country, solemnly.

"My fellow Americans, news just reached my office that the Polish capital, Warsaw was struck by multiple, medium-range missiles, presumably fired from Russian soil.

"Numerous buildings in the Sejm and Senate Complex, home to both houses of the Polish Parliament, were destroyed. At present, we do not have an exact account of dead and injured.

"The historic Presidential Palace, residence of Polish President, Bazyli Woycik, has sustained grave damage and, at present, the fate of the President and his family is unknown. We pray for their safety.

The screen flashed to images of Warsaw in flames.

Most of the world was not old enough to recall the scenes of German stormtroopers reducing the city to a comparable pile of rubble, but Hyden was not going to let a tragedy go to waste.

"These attacks come on the heels of verification by the UN inspectors that the fragments of the short range missiles used in the Włodawa assault were indeed Russian in origin.

"We must assume, if these attacks are not sanctioned by Russian President Kirill Golubev, rogue elements of his military are acting beyond his control, and he is no longer in charge of the Kremlin."

Hyden paused to let America see his well-rehearsed somber face, while that frightening thought sank into the collective psyche.

"As I address you, members of U.S. Land Forces V Corps Forward Command are being dispatched from their base in Poznań, Poland to Warsaw to assist in search and rescue, while additional forces are being deployed along border between Poland and the Russian semi-exclave of Kaliningrad Oblast, and that of Belarus.

"Our Scandinavian NATO allies, Norway, Finland, and our friends in Sweden, are patrolling the Baltic Sea to ensure neither the Russian Fleet nor their submarines will be able to enter the Atlantic.

"Not since 1962 when President John F. Kennedy was confronted with the dire possibility of a global nuclear holocaust, have we as a country confronted such grave conditions.

"Our bases across the globe have been placed on DEFCON Two, while our forward bases in Europe have been raised to DEFCON One.

"I come before you to reassure, America will not fire the first shot, unless we are given no other choice. I ask each of you to attend your chosen house of worship and pray for peace. We in Washington are working diligently to prevent this from escalating.

"With that, I bid you goodnight."

No sooner had Hyden faded from the screen, than the game's commentator roared, "Can you believe that kickoff run? It's reminiscent of the wild, early days of the league.

"With all of the laterals and missed tackles, I don't think anyone in NFL history has ever seen quite a trick play like that. I know the home crowd is still stunned by what they witnessed. It's definitely a game changer for DC.

"Checking the replay, not even our cameramen were able to follow it all.

"I guarantee, you'll never see anything like that again."

The next day, the New York Stock Market jumped nine-hundred and twenty-two points on the strength of the Military Complex's stocks.

As for Hyden's approval ratings, he went from 29 to 38. Even the critics in his party voiced their support for his cautious but firm handling of the situation.

While the boost in his numbers did not guarantee his nomination, it did make him a strongly viable candidate, and donations shifted from a slow trickle to a reasonably steady flow.

CHAPTER TWELVE

"Listen, you damn bastard," Kira swore at Leo. "How could you, let alone your country, make me look like such a fool in front of the world? I bought your bullshit hook, line, and sinker. I printed everything just like you and Mikhaylov wanted. I even went before Congress to defend your stupid asses.

"Then what do you go and do? You turn around and do the exact same thing and lob more missiles at Poland, into the heart of Warsaw, no less. I hope the Poles—"

Her castigation fell on deaf ears. Kira heard Leo yelling at somebody else in the room, ignoring her rant completely.

"God dammit, I don't care if the general is in his hot tub with the entire Bolshoi Ballet, get his ass in here now. I need those tanks moved out of Ukraine and repositioned along the Belarus-Polish border before NATO rolls into Red Square."

A muffled voice in the background charged, "But, sir, you *do not* have the authority to surrender our gains in that country to the Fascist Gangsters in Kyiv."

"Don't call it a surrender. Consider it a strategic truce,

allowing those overstuffed uniforms in the Kremlin to save face while we save the country."

"Leo—" Kira raised her voice.

"For the last time, Kira, I don't have time to deal with you. Why do you always contact me when it is least convenient?"

"Because I know you'll be in the office?" she wise cracked, hoping to ease some of the tension.

Hearing nothing in reply, she continued, "As I've been trying to tell you, the American soldier did not commit suicide. Someone threw him over the balcony."

"Right now, I do not care if he was shot out of a circus cannon. Unless you can tell me who is firing missiles at the Poles, and I doubt that would be your dead Corporal, we are done. Good day."

The line went dead.

Kira stared at her cell, thinking about the conversation… or lack thereof.

Leo should have disconnected the call before he began issuing orders. He had not.

Was he trying to get a message across about troop movements and the gravity of the situation?

Hell, he just revealed the Russians were abandoning the vast expanse of Ukraine for which they had sacrificed more than thirty-thousand troops and countless billions in equipment trying to take.

If Mikhaylov already knew the autopsy results of Corporal Davis, I'm positive Leo did as well.

What did it mean?

Kira's next call was to Lieutenant Juan Hernández. Succinctly, and without revealing her sources, she repeated the conversations she had with Leo and Fyodor.

No matter how strategically she phrased her words, it

sounded as though she were relaying a direct communique from Moscow.

Taking a breath, she concluded, "Does that qualify as enough pertinent information? *Now* will you take me to Lejeune?"

"What do you hope to accomplish there?" Juan asked.

"I want to interview the CO…" Kira flipped through her paperwork. "…Baxter's his name. I am hoping to find out what they discovered about Davis being AWOL."

"I can save you a trip then. Baxter was transferred last week to Gitmo—"

"As in Guantanamo Bay Naval Base, Cuba?"

"Unless you know another and, I can guarantee, without Presidential authorization, you are not getting access to that base."

"Why the hell did he get sent there?"

"Can't tell you. Maybe he pissed in somebody's corn-flakes. What I *can* tell you is, the night Davis disappeared, he, Davis, not Baxter, was scheduled to stand guard duty. Failed to show up."

Juan added a curious observation, "Hmm, this is odd. A base wide search was implemented for him immediately, which included a search of his locker and chest. The only items missing were a set of civilian clothes."

"What's so strange about that? I doubt he'd be packing for a long term vacation."

"It's not what he took or left that's peculiar, it's how quickly the MPs were dispatched to look for him. Almost as if someone already knew he wouldn't be found."

"Does it say anything in your notes about his grand-mother dying?"

"Only a footnote about a possible overdose, and being overcome by her gas stove, which she had left on…"

Over the line, Kira heard the rustle of papers being thumbed through.

"…and that she was a Do Not Resuscitate."

"Funny thing about that, no one remembers her ever signing one," Kira countered. "Not to mention, the suicide she supposedly committed was one hundred and eighty degrees out of character."

"What are you saying, Kira?"

"Somebody murdered the old woman and tried to cover it up."

"What proof do you have of that?" Juan could not help but ask.

"According to my source—"

"No doubt another anonymous one?"

Ignoring the snide comment, Kira repeated, "According to my source, who knew Mrs. Davis personally, no one remembered her completing a DNR at any time, yet it popped up in her medical records the day she died, on top of the fact that, to her, the idea of suicide was an unforgivable sin."

"You do realize, Kira, you're seeing conspiracies everywhere you look?"

"Look at the evidence, Juan. This is beginning to scream government—"

"Before you finish that sentence, who are you trying to accuse? What purpose would framing some kid from Iowa serve?"

"To hide the true identities."

"Who are?"

"I'm not ready to name names."

"That sounds like bullshit to me. Tell me your thoughts."

"Nope, because you'll send the guys with nets after me if I do."

"I still may. Haven't decided whether you're a danger to the country, or just yourself."

Preparing to give her antagonizing ex, a smart comeback… even if he *did* have a valid point, and sounded slightly concerned for her safety, another call derailed Kira's train of thought.

A glance at the screen informed her it was from Vice President Hernández.

Kira had hesitated to contact Stefi after Hyden's masterful preempting of her friend's presidential aspirations. While she wanted to commiserate, Kira was afraid anything she might say would sound like a reporter's question and set off an emotional landmine.

While Kira held zero respect for either Hyden's leadership or ethics, she had to give him kudos for knowing how to play cutthroat politics. Knocking Stefi off the television with such an important message, effectively cut into any gains she might have hoped to garner.

"Hey, Juan, your crazy sister is calling," she said with a slight chuckle. "I guess, technically, she outranks you, so I should answer it."

"Yeah, whatever, Kira. Just take care of yourself."

Switching the contacts, Kira answered, "Hey, girl. I'm sorry, I haven't called in a couple. That was pure bull—"

"Shut up and get out of your place, now!"

"No, wait, I need to tell you what my sources had to say. It's solid intel you need to hear."

"Don't say another word. Just run. My NSA geek told me they've been eavesdropping on—"

The warning came too late.

Kira's front door met an untimely demise at the end of a battering ram as an FBI SWAT team, in black riot gear and holding M4 carbine rifles, burst into her apartment.

"What the fuck?" Kira fumed, as one of the squad

snatched the phone from her hand, and two more pinned her to the floor.

"Kira Monroe," began the agent who grabbed her phone and was now standing over her. "You are under arrest for suspicion of espionage against the United States of America."

"Are you crazy?" Kira retaliated. "What right do you have to do this?"

"Sections 703 and 704, Title VII, of the Foreign Intelligence Surveillance Act. Now, shut up and come along—"

"We both know FISA is unconstitutional as hell. I demand my right to my attorney."

"Right now, you have no rights, except what I feel like giving you, and that's not much."

Kira was hauled to her feet, her infuriated gaze clashing with a pair of implacable dark eyes peering through a black balaclava.

He signaled to the two on either side of Kira to remove her from the premises.

Wrists cuffed behind her back, her ignominious exit took her passed a line of similarly dressed agents, carrying boxes into her apartment. She assumed they were going to confiscate her evidence, meager as it was.

Over her shoulder, she muttered, "You'll all pay for this."

Pulling a hood from his pocket and yanking it over Kira's head, successfully blinding her, the one who appeared to be in charge, retorted, "I can't wait."

From her fifth-floor home, she was marched downstairs in full view of her fellow tenants. Kira heard them confirming what they *always* suspected in self-satisfied whispers.

Outside, she was manhandled into the back of a vehicle — which, she supposed, must be some sort of prison truck — idling in front of her building.

A chain harness was cinched around her waist and

shackled to the bench she was obliged to sit on, holding her almost immobile.

Kira heard the inner cage clang shut, followed by the outer doors.

The engine revved and, with a jolt, the truck lurched forward.

CHAPTER THIRTEEN

The ride in the back of the truck was as uncomfortable as it was eerily silent, prompting Kira to speculate whether the caged portion of the vehicle was soundproofed.

She tried to focus on any noises filtering through from the other side of the truck's walls, but it was impossible to distinguish anything useful.

Without her cell phone, she lost track of time. The only accurate judge of its passage, the creeping numbness in her fingers.

Whichever ass had cuffed her, had secured them too tightly, restricting the flow of blood to her hands. The more she flexed them, the worse it got.

She tried driving her thumb nail into the pad of her middle finger but felt nothing, becoming concerned, if this ride continued much longer, she would lose her fingers all together.

As she contemplated a life lacking the ability to use a computer keyboard, the truck came to an abrupt stop, jerking her to the right. The chain on her left snapped taut, causing the harness to bite into her right side between her lower rib and her hip. The unexpected pain forced the air from her lungs, and caused stars to dance in front of her eyes.

The doors of the vehicle swung open, ushering the fresh scent of manure. *Am I in the Virginia countryside? Fauquier or Loudoun county?*

She heard a bell ring, followed by the thunder of hooves pounding into fleshly turned dirt and people whooping in excitement.

Oh my God, am I in Charles Town, West Virginia? Why the hell bring me here?

She had no time to consider her predicament before she was lifted bodily from the truck and frog-marched across a graveled area. Pebbles skipped and bounced off her ankles and shins as she tried to keep up with her captors, hampered by not being able to see where she was putting her feet.

The agents came to a halt. Hearing more horses whinnying, and stomping about, led her to suspect she was close to or inside one of the stables.

The prickly bulk they sat her on, had to be a bale of hay — confirmed when one of the men removed the hood, and left her in the dimly lit barn.

Her eyes adjusting, Kira discovered she was in a stall behind a man who was grooming a beautiful, flaxen-chestnut thoroughbred. The overwhelming temptation to stroke the creature's nose, was only thwarted because she was restrained.

Without stopping his task or turning, the man addressed her, "Miss Monroe, do you fancy yourself a horse lover?"

Even with his back to her, she recognized the voice, "No, Director Sullivan, I can't say I'm much of a pet person at all."

"What a pity. Horses are such beautiful creatures, willing to be broken with relative ease under the right hand, much like women used to be. Though their loyalty is greater than any human could understand, and prepared to run themselves to death at the whim of their rider."

Putting his brush on a stool, he faced Kira.

"I don't suppose you would be that loyal for the sake of your country, would you?"

"While I appreciate losing my security deposit because of your goons and being kidnapped so you can provide a lesson in animal husbandry, I fail to understand why we are not having this discussion in your office or, at the very least, on the phone?" she prevaricated.

"Let's just call this a private meeting. Away from recording devices and interfering lawyers."

"But why *West Virginia* of all places?"

The question earned Kira a chuckle. "I expected you, of all people, to know the Eastern Panhandle is the home of our shadow government. While most of this state knows it, they don't care because we pay well."

"So am I to guess your master ordered this?"

"Now, now, Kira… may I call you Kira?"

"No," Kira rebuffed.

Sullivan shrugged and continued, "If you are referring to the President, he has more important matters to contend with than the likes of you. Which means it falls to me to clarify governmental policies which are above your paygrade or understanding.

"You need to take a step back, and choose other topics to submit to that rag you work for. You are dangerously close to divulging information which could be construed as aiding the enemy."

"Enemy? Does that not imply we are in direct conflict with the Russians?"

"Oh, how remiss of me. I had forgotten you spent the last few hours joyriding around Virginias."

"Stop beating around the bush, Sullivan, and spit it out."

Sullivan broke into a crooked grin. "In your absence, a contingency of NATO coalition forces crossed into Russia from Poland, via northern Belarus, led by Polish General Jakub Krol of the Polish First Division. I'm happy to say the Belarus army rolled over and played dead.

"NATO agreed with the Poles that it was a necessary tactic before the Russians reinforced their rear guard with the tanks, *you* thoughtfully informed us, were being moved from Ukraine. It is unlikely the majority will reach their destination because the Ukrainians have been chasing them across Belarus, by land and air."

"What in God's name have you done, and why tell me? You know if I get out of here, I'm going to print everything you just told me."

"Doesn't really matter now, does it? Your reputation as a *bona fide* journalist took a massive hit by your own hand with your stunt in front of Congress. Chances are, your arrest for being a possible Russian operative is following on its heels throughout cable news."

Kira blanched, acknowledging the significance of his words.

"As for your *lover*," Sullivan's assumption dripped with sarcasm. "The Russian FSD received an anonymous tip off about him. I doubt his treatment will be as gentle as yours. They do not suffer traitors gladly."

A painful knot formed in Kira's chest. That Sullivan's information was out of date, did not make the notion of Leo being tortured, or worse, because of his association with her, any less painful. *Protect him,* she begged the universe.

Picking up his brush, Sullivan resumed the rhythmic grooming of his horse.

"The ol' girl here is running her last race today," he said, offhandedly. "Take a lesson from her experience and know when to quit. One final piece of advice. Before you do any more damage to your friend's aspirations, I'd recommend giving her a wide berth. Wouldn't look good for a Presidential candidate to be associated with an enemy spy… given current events."

He finished his counselling session, at the same moment as the two men returned and tugged Kira upright.

Refusing to budge or be cowed, she planted her feet. "Mr. Director do not be foolish enough to imagine this is enough to scare me off. I will see you and that bastard Hyden behind bars."

"If you are thinking of trying to connect the little dust-up in Europe to our President, might as well forget that, too. You forget who runs the domestic legal arm of the US government; I doubt it will gain any traction."

Eastern Europe

Flying captured Su-35 Russian jets, the Ukrainian air wing, nicknamed the *Ghost Squadron*, sped across the night sky towards Minsk.

The planes bore the Russian Air Force insignias, a ploy they had learned from the invading Russians in the early days of the Russian-Ukrainian war, minus the ridiculous *Z* painted on their vertical stabilizers. The Ukrainian pilots prided themselves on being able to tell friend from foe.

Before pinning the Belarus Air Force to their bases around the capital, they had sharpened their skills in the Russian aircraft, sweeping through the columns of tanks trapped on the M8 motorway, between the Belarus-Ukraine border and the southern Belarus city of Gomel.

The lead tanks were reduced to burning rubble, while the

American-made M1A2 Abrams tanks, *on lease* from Poland, ate their way through the rear echelons.

Russian General Petrov Peshkov — a descendant of Maxim Gorky, the famed Russian author and political activist, forever immortalized in the name of a certain Moscow park — squinted through his night vision monocular, to discern what remained of his tank squadrons. The fires blazing fore and aft made it almost impossible to see clearly.

He murmured a prayer just loud enough for those in his tank to hear, "God, grant us the miracle of life and deliver us the Polish border so we can disrupt that damn column of NATO tanks and save our country."

While the Russian reinforcements battled their way north, divisions of the Belarus Special Operations Forces fought their way South, in an attempt to relieve the beleaguered Russian troops and expel the Ukrainians.

The bulk of the Belarus armed forces refused to join the fight, citing Russian aggression against its neighbors as justification for the mutiny, not even the threat of death from the elected dictator triggered any movement.

While vengeance rained down on the Russian forces in Southern Belarus, the coalition troops had cut across the north of the country, and entered Russian soil.

Theoretically, Russia had already lost land when the Second Polish Brigade rolled over the Kaliningrad-Oblast border, reclaiming the area as its own and officially reverting the city's name to the Polish, Krolewiec.

The remnants of the government in Warsaw who survived the missile attack, had made a deal with Berlin to avert any chance of the Germans renouncing *The Final Settle-ment Agreement* of 1990, and reclaiming what was, histori-cally, their coronation city of Königsberg until its annexation by the Soviet Union in 1945, thus preventing any discontent among the allies.

General Krol received the happy news of the Oblast's fall while en route to the Russian city of Smolensk. Being early October, the general knew they had to move quickly to reach Moscow before the winter snows stalled any hope of progress.

As the tank columns rumbled eastward, Krol heard his radio operator exclaim into his headphones, "General, Sir, you need to hear this."

Krol heard the radio crackle then clear for the voice of Russian President Kirill Golubev.

Golubev spoke with almost unnerving calm, "To the invaders from the West, I have authorized the use of tactical nuclear missiles, if you do not cease your hostilities and vacate the territories seized from Mother Russia and our ally, Belarus.

"You have twenty-four hours from this announcement to return to the Polish Frontier.

"Do not be so foolish as to view the deadline as a sign of weakness. As with Napoleon and the French, and Hitler and his Nazis, we Russians will teach you, we are not afraid to sacrifice the few for the sake of the many.

"The difference now, compared with then, is how far we are willing to extend our Scorched Earth Policy.

"Consider this your only warning."

The announcement was followed by a rendition of Tchaikovsky's *1812 Overture*, performed by the Russian National Orchestra complete with church bells and cannons, then the Russian National Anthem.

After which, the radio went silent.

The twenty minute musical interlude faded into the rumble of the tank's gas turbine engine.

Krol's headset sputtered to life again, this time relaying the distinct baritone of the American Colonel, who's squadron was assigned to the rear.

"General Krol?" the man asked in his slow Texas accent. "Do we halt our progress, sir, or return to the bases?"

"Our orders have not changed and we are allies. If you and your men plan to, how do you Americans put it so eloquently… turn tail and run, that is on you.

"As for me, we are less than three hundred miles from Moscow, and I intend to rectify a thousand years of Polish humiliation at the hands of the East Slavic barbarians.

"If you believe Golubev is willing to turn his farmland into a radioactive deathtrap, you are a fool. It is just more Russian propaganda."

CHAPTER FOURTEEN

Washington, D.C.

The return trip to DC was less uncomfortable for Kira. Instead of being manhandled into the truck, she was permitted the middle seat of the van.

Her attempts to converse with the men, hoping to gain any information concerning her arrest or the recent eruption of war in Eastern Europe, failed to garner a single response.

Arriving at the front of her building, the driver decelerated long enough for one of his colleagues to push her out of the side door.

Stumbling, but refusing to fall on her face, Kira swung around and flipped the van the bird as it roared off.

The elevator ride up was almost as awkward as the march down the staircase. Four of Kira's neighbors who shared the lift, most of whom would normally greet her and exchange obligatory small talk, ignored the young journalist as completely as though she did not exist. Not one even deigned to glance her way.

Reaching her apartment, Kira discovered a sheet of

plywood nailed across the gap in place of her door. Affixed to the panel was a thirty-day eviction notice, citing… as justi-fication… property damage, disturbing other tenants, and irreparable harm to the complex's reputation.

Kira huffed angrily, "You want to see damage?"

Descending to the basement, she dug through her box of tools stored there. Returning to the wooden barrier, she jammed a heavy metal crowbar between doorframe and plywood, and began prying them apart.

It took a good twenty-minutes, ably assisted by an inordinate amount of rage-driven strength but, at last, the panel lay in pieces in the hallway.

Propping the crowbar against the wall, she entered her home to find it in complete disarray. Her furniture was overturned. Cushions ripped open. Books, in varying states of manhandling, discarded haphazardly across the floor. Even her lingerie drawer had been rifled through.

"Jesus, if you were looking for any IUDs, you should have just checked my toy drawer instead," Kira said to the upheaval in her bedroom.

Acknowledging, she had to face it, and trying to ignore a sense of trepidation, Kira went along the hall to her office.

This door too, hung off its frame. Papers were strewn everywhere, and her laptop was missing all together.

The photographs of her great-grandfather and other family members no longer adorned the walls. Kira knew what they were looking for but, hopefully, did not find.

Crossing to her bookcase, she examined it for any obvious indication the FBI had *inspected* it. Handcrafted for the patriarch of the Monroe family when on assignment in London during World War II and becoming a treasured family heirloom, the cabinet showed signs of age and use, but no scarring caused by brutal tools.

Her great-grandfather had designed the piece of furniture

with the help of a skilled White Chapel carpenter who built it in his shop.

Slipping her hand down the panel closest to the wall, Kira pressed on the bottom molding, releasing a small drawer secreted therein.

Ned feared the English would succumb to the German onslaught before America abandoned its policy of neutrality and got off its ass to join the war. He had the drawer installed hoping to prevent his notes and observations from falling into Nazi hands.

Kira's father had also concealed a collection of documents in the hidden drawer — the contents to which she was never privy, because Robert had ensured their destruction shortly before his death.

Now, it served as a storage receptacle for the multiple thumb drives, she used to back up her files. Her old man had drilled into her, until it became a mantra, the importance of making copies of her work early and often.

While she had not the time to record the conversations before the horde of unwanted visitors descended, she *had* made copies of everything else. Scooping them out, she dumped them in her pocket, to be sorted through when she had access to a computer.

"Fuckers," Kira groused. "Just wait 'til I burn you all."

The same drawer housed a few old photographs, and she flipped through them; black and white shots her mom had taken of her family when they were in the Middle East.

One made her laugh. She was with her dad at the pyramids, riding a camel led by local guide. Her dad looked as though the camel was making him seasick.

As she replaced them, her fingers brushed two metal cylinders. Even without looking at them, Kira knew these were the Cuban Cohiba Cigars her dad had bought when she graduated from journalism school and was hired by Unified

Media. Kira had managed about three puffs before she turned green.

Behind the cigars, rested a wooden box.

Extracting it carefully, she set it on the floor and flipped the worn clasp.

Lifting the lid, she marveled at the Makarov PM pistol inside. The family legend held that her mom had purchased it from a Berlin pawn broker shortly after the fall of the Berlin Wall.

The man claimed its former owner was a member of the East German Stasi who had used it to shoot a man attempting to escape over the wall.

Her mom had not cared.

She bought it because she understood it was one of the easiest weapons to conceal, insisting her husband carry it whenever he was on assignment.

Neither parent ever verified the story. Reporters were not supposed to be armed, especially in a war zone.

Kira lifted it from the box and tested its weight in her hand. At a little over a pound and a half, concealing it would be no problem, nor would drawing it quickly, if necessary.

Robert had kept the pistol in pristine condition. Even now, the slide moved smoothly, thanks, in part, to the replacement he had ordered directly from the manufacturer in Russia. The amount of pressure needed to pull the trigger was still light.

Loading one of the .380 caliber magazines into the grip, she tucked the other in her pocket.

"Nobody is going to get the best of me this time."

Changing into jeans and a sweater, which had not suffered the same fate as her front door, Kira dug around the debris until she found her satchel. Thankfully, her credit cards were inside, but whether they had been deactivated by the FBI or NSA was another question.

Slinging the bag over her shoulder, she trudged through the destroyed doorframe, pausing long enough to lean the door in place, ordering it to, "Stay."

As she stepped into the elevator, she heard it fall with a solid **thud** to the floor. Not bothering to look back, she pressed the button and headed to the ground floor.

Kira used the cab ride to the Farragut Center to ease her nerves. Her hand brushed against the pistol in her pocket, reassured she had a chance to fight back.

The driver drew up to the building where Kira expected to find a modicum of sanctuary. Home to Unified Media… here, she ought to be untouchable.

A notion shattered the moment she entered the office.

No sooner had she walked onto the fourth floor, than all eyes swiveled in her direction. She tried not to pay attention, but the whispers, and finger pointing caught in her peripheral vision, made it impossible.

Reaching her desk, she sat down and removed the thumb drives, to check the data on each.

Her computer screen came up, asking for her password. She typed in *CIAKilledKennedy1963* and hit enter as usual.

Instead of granting her access, it asked for a valid password. She keyed in her password again, only to be denied a second, and then a third time. A screen popped up informing her, she was locked out of her account and to contact the Administrator.

She picked up the phone, preparing to rail at IT about its ineptitude when Walter appeared at her desk, taking the phone from her hand, and replacing it on the cradle.

A hint of confusion clouded Kira's eyes as she met his gaze.

"Walter, what gives? I've got the story of the century, hell, the millennium, and I can't get on my computer to piece it together."

"Miss Monroe—"

"Miss what? I don't have time to be screwing around with—"

"It pains me to inform you, your services are no longer welcome within any of the offices of Unified Media International."

"Walter, please. Don't tell me, Hyden has gotten to you as well."

Ignoring her plea, Walter continued with the script he was given to memorize the moment UMI's CEO had received the call from the White House and the Justice Department threatening legal action if Kira Monroe was not fired forthwith.

"Your behaviour in front of Congress, streamed live I might add, was unprofessional and left a poor impression upon the other—"

"That seems to be a common complaint," Kira interjected sourly.

"—journalists in our employment. Likewise, your recent arrest, also televised live, put an end to any credibility you may have possessed."

There it was… Sullivan's threat brought to fruition.

"Walter, listen to me. Sullivan had me kidnapped under the guise of being arrested, which allowed the FBI to ransack my home. Sullivan dragged my ass to West Virginia to intimidate me and keep me out—"

Walter held up his palm to stop her uttering another word. Stepping to one side, he summoned the burly security guards, whose approach Kira had not detected.

"Gentlemen please escort Miss Monroe from the building, and make sure she does not take any Media property with her, including those flash drives on the desk."

He pulled a notepad from his pocket, and flipped it open. "The company will ship your belongings to your address—"

His pencil froze mid-air at the distinct sound of a gun's hammer clicking into place. Nervously, he looked up to realize he was staring down the barrel of a small gun. An apprehensive twitch tugged at the edges of his cheeks as he tried to play it off with a grin.

Kira had not planned to pull the Makarov from her pocket; it was sheer instinct, especially after the events of the day but, now it was in full view, she had no intention of backing down.

"C-Come on now, Kira—"

"Oh, it's Kira again, is it? Does that mean we're back to being friends and you're not sacking me?"

"Y-you have to understand, it's not up to me. The decision came down the food chain."

"That's what I thought. So, this is what's going to happen. I'm taking the drives with me. I paid for them with the paltry wages, I earned here. As for the two gorillas, tell them to stand aside, and nobody will get hurt."

Security did not need to be told twice. Both raised their hands and moved out of Kira's way.

Gathering the drives from the desk, she dropped them into her satchel.

Pushing past the three, she informed Walter, "Make sure to inform your boss that when this story comes out, he won't be spared either."

Her ultimatum burning her final bridge at Unified Media International, Kira stalked to the exit, back ramrod straight, head held high, aware everyone in the office was videoing the confrontation on their cell phones… or calling 911.

It mattered not. By the time the police arrived, she would

be long gone, leaving UMI with more than enough footage to make her the lead story for yet another night.

What *did* scare her was the thought of being arrested again as a psychotic terrorist. It was doubtful even Stefi could pull enough strings to save her from that.

CHAPTER FIFTEEN

Without a computer, Kira had no alternative but to go to the nearest electronics store to look for a replacement. Cash was in short supply, and her credit cards were nearly maxed out. She hoped she had the wherewithal to purchase one with sufficient capacity to access the portable drives, so she could complete her story.

No sooner had Kira walked through the front door, than a salesman, who looked scarcely old enough to shave let alone know crap about technology, approached.

"Welcome to Best Circuits, your complete electronic and computer supercenter. I'm Rick, what can I set you up with today?"

"Geez, do you say that to everyone?" Kira could not help but chuckle.

"If I want to get paid, I do. Now, whatcha need?"

"Well, I could use a nice laptop, but don't think I can afford one."

Rick smiled. "Let me worry about that. We have credit. Why don't we run yours to see what we can send you out the door with."

Shrugging, Kira agreed.

After filling out the application, Rick suggested, "Go look around and I'll be with you in a moment."

With a knowing grin, he left her in front of the most expensive computers on offer.

She toyed around with some of the keyboards, glancing at the salesman every now and then who, in turn, was watching her, an odd expression on his face.

"That's strange," he said when he came back to her. "They could not find a credit report on you. I'm sure it's some sort of computer glitch."

Before Kira could respond, she was escorted to the door.

"I'll tell you what, I have your address. We'll send you a response in the mail within the next week to ten days."

Back on the sidewalk, she stared through the glass frontage in disbelief. Treating the formerly friendly salesman to an obscene gesture, Kira stomped off.

Fortuitously, at the corner of the street, there was an internet cafe. Ordering a cup of coffee, Kira spent some time researching herself.

First, she logged into the three credit reporting companies. Each one listed her social security number as invalid. She moved on to her credit cards.

All were flagged, *Invalid Account*. It was not that they were closed, it was as though they had never existed. While being debt free ought to feel exhilarating, the idea she might become a nonperson was profoundly disturbing.

"No doubt by the dirty fingers of FBI Director Sullivan," Kira muttered at the screen. Though, in truth, any number of Intelligence or Security Services across Europe could be responsible for her dilemma.

Her only alternative was the site her father had instructed her not to access unless it was a dire emergency. While he never trusted the American government, a hidden account via a Dark Web bank seemed extreme, even for him.

Rummaging in her satchel, Kira retrieved her worn address book. Thumbing through the pages, she stopped at the F section, and ran down the listings until she came to *Figueroa, Roseanne* — her mother's maiden name. The corresponding number was 00493077509213.

To the casual observer, it appeared to be a German phone number. Her mom had decided to remain in Berlin after her husband's death.

Kira hesitated to bring up the site, convinced it was a hoax. Knowing her dad, it could be something as benign as a pop-up screen tossing confetti and shouting, **Surprise**, to some weird online porn platform.

Warily, Kira typed in the address she had, at her father's insistence, committed to memory, expecting every computer in the place to go black and then spontaneously burst into flames.

A small mustachioed man appeared on the screen and asked, "Number please?"

Kira keyed in the 'phone number' assigned to her mom. The man vanished, reappearing seconds later holding a cartoon-esque money bag.

Stamped on the bag: $25000.

Dumbfounded, she gaped at the screen.

Did Dad really squirrel away all this money for me?

The cartoon man's face expanded until it filled the entire screen. In an equally anime-like voice, he said, "Would you like it sent to Alexandria Branch? Yes or No?"

She pressed the *Y* key and, instantly, a sheet spat out from the adjacent printer. It provided a street address, and nothing else.

"You are expected to arrive at our doors within forty-five minutes or your prize will be forfeit."

A small mushroom cloud melted his friendly face into a burning skull, and then the screen went black.

Someone walking passed remarked, "Cool game. Something you're creating?"

Scooting from her chair, she replied airily, "Yeah, something like that."

It took Kira ten minutes to flag down a cab and another thirty to travel down George Washington Memorial Parkway to Old Town Alexandria, Virginia. Nerves getting the better of her, she kept checking her watch, certain they would not reach the destination in time.

The driver parked in front of a vacant lot. "Are you sure you have the right address, lady?" he asked cynically. "Doesn't look like there's been anything here but a homeless camp for years."

Kira's heart sank. *Dad, how could you have been so cruel?*

Suddenly, the rear passenger side door opened, and a shabbily dressed man climbed in next to Kira, ordering the cabbie to, "Drive, and the pair of you look straight ahead."

"Get out of my cab," the driver snarled.

The man flashed a large pistol tucked inside of his coat.

"You're the boss," the driver complied without further argument.

They drew away from the curb and cruised down the street, in no particular direction.

Afraid to do anything except follow the stranger's instructions, Kira fixed her gaze on the back of the driver's head. Doubtless, they would end up dead somewhere in the hinterland of Virginia.

Her fingers grazed over the pistol in her pocket aware he had not noticed it. *If it's a gunfight the bastard wants, that's what he'll get.*

The cab rolled up to the second stoplight. The occupants heard the passenger door open and close. They turned to see an empty seat. The man had vanished into traffic.

Kira reached out to her right, her hand landing on a brown paper bag, which crunched under her fingertips. Peeking inside, she spied stacks of twenties and hundreds, bound neatly.

"Farragut Center, please," Kira asked.

"Like hell. Get out."

A nearby convenience store lived up to its reputation. Kira spotted a rack of cheap burner phones. Purchasing a handful, she tossed all but one into her shoulder bag, where they joined the bundles of cash.

She programmed a neon green flip phone and called the only number she could trust.

"Go for Executive Programmer Francisco Diaz," a cheery voice on the other end answered.

"Cisco, it's Kira."

"Jesus, Kira, where the hell are you? What's this I hear about you threatening the lives of your co-workers? The cops have a warrant out for your arrest and have you listed as armed and dangerous."

"Cisco, shut up and listen. I can't be sure if your line is tapped. I need you—"

"Kira, you know I'd do anything for you, but Stefi is in New Hampshire campaigning so I can't get a hold of her."

Growling, Kira said, "Last time… shut up and visit your abuela."

"My abuela? W-why is she sick?"

Checking her watch, Kira hung up before answering.

She placed one more call to a cab company before she took the sim chip out of the phone and destroyed both.

Kira tipped the driver well to remain parked up the street from the Victorian house in the heart of Columbia Heights. From her position she saw Cisco's sky blue Camry.

What a yuppie, she giggled inwardly.

Waiting until she was certain, he had not been followed to his grandmother's place, Kira prepared to alight from the back seat.

Suddenly, two black SUV's barreled up the street, squealing to a stop in front of the house. A cadre of agents emptied out of the vehicles and surrounded the house, guns drawn.

One climbed the wooden steps to Grandma Emilia's front door, pounding on it with his fist.

He yelled so loudly, even Kira could hear, "FBI, open the door. We know you are harboring a wanted fugitive. Open up now, or we'll be forced to break the door down."

A frail-looking woman, slightly hunched from years of cleaning rich people's houses to ensure her children and grandchildren had a proper education, opened the door, and stepped onto the porch. She let the screen door slam behind her as though to emphasize her presence.

Anger flared in eyes as she forced her body upright to face the agent. Cisco had managed to give her a quick explanation for his sudden visit before these bastards dared to darken her doorstep.

Emilia had met Kira only a few times, but her grandson liked her, as did his fiancé, Estefanía, whom Emilia loved — their recent engagement pleasing her immensely.

"Sir," the elderly lady began, "if you are in possession of a search warrant, you are welcome to enter my house and look around...*peacefully*. If you do not, I suggest you scurry back to whatever corrupt judge you use and get one.

"In either case, you will not find Kira Monroe. The girl is too smart to be caught here, and was only testing the extent of your illegal wiretaps.

"Looks like you walked right in her trap."

She held the door open for the man repeating, "Do you have a warrant or not?"

The man smacked the paperwork against Emillia's chest before entering her house, followed by an army of FBI agents.

The old woman sniped, "Pendejos."

Slipping another hundred dollar bill through the sliding glass, Kira instructed the driver, "Take me to the Library of Congress."

The driver glanced between the parade of agents and the proffered money. Greed being the greater motivator, he snatched the note, and shifted the car into gear.

He heard his fare swear from the backseat, "Shit, I still need a laptop."

"Might I stop at my cousin Sid's pawnshop? He doesn't ask a lot of the questions, though he probably should. It's a little out of the way, if you don't mind a side trip."

"Sure," Kira said in resignation. "How much more can an additional charge for possession of stolen merchandise hurt?"

CHAPTER SIXTEEN

On the way to Sid's shop — which wasn't so much a storefront as a garage tucked between warehouses along the road to the Washington Metropolitan Area Rail Yard, TJ — Kira's new personal chauffeur — had detoured past the depot to drop off his cab and pick up his own car.

He used some of the money, Kira had bribed him with, to buy them a bite to eat from a local diner, pointing out, "You look starved half to death. My Momma would slap the shit out of me if I didn't feed you."

"You have a smart mom," Kira mumbled around a turkey and cheese sub.

"Maybe so," TJ replied, "but dontcha dare drop any mayo on my seat." He ran his hand over the worn, burgundy, velour upholstery of his 1979 Oldsmobile 88. "She's a classic you know."

"Yeah, yeah." Kira smiled. "I'll be careful."

Pulling up to the shop's 'frontage', TJ honked the horn, magically triggering the garage opener. Once the Oldsmobile had slipped inside, Sid poked his head outside to check for any cops then closed the shutter.

TJ had hardly opened the car door when the aforementioned Sid flew into a rant, "Goddamn it, TJ, you know you're not supposed to bring strangers here. How do you know she's not an undercover cop? Jesus, man, do you want me to send me back to jail?"

"Chill, man," TJ interrupted, tossing a wrapped sub at his cousin. "The lady here is in more trouble than your garbage hole could ever generate. Feds are chasing her."

"Oh, great, that's even worse." Sid griped through his mouthful as he pushed past the two. "What is she looking for, besides trouble?"

"Hey," Kira finally got a word in edgewise. "*She* can answer for herself."

Sid stopped in his tracks, spun on his boot, and feigned a bow. "Pardon me, your highness, how may this humble merchant be of service?"

"TJ, fuck this guy. I don't care if he is your cousin, I don't need his attitude."

TJ was about to apologize for Sid's personality, but his cousin beat him to the punch, "You may not need my attitude, but you being here, tells me you need one of my laptop specials."

Sid's perception impressed Kira, not that she was about to let him know.

"Something with a built-in VPN so the Feds can't track you? Maybe a jailbroken operating system, so none of the *trustworthy* operating systems can report you either?"

Sid disappeared behind a glass case, which had seen better days, and the pair heard him rummaging somewhere beneath the display units.

He placed a military grade laptop on the glass top. It was bulkier than Kira was looking for, but the shell screamed its ability to survive if dropped from a decent height and, that it had been tested thoroughly, verified by the numerous scratches.

"How hot is it?"

"You cut me to the quick. It isn't. Belonged to a hacker friend of mine who upgraded." Sid shrugged. "He wiped it of everything, except the operating system and the VPN program.

"Anyway, yours for 5K."

"Come on, Sid," TJ groused. "You're losing it. Give Kira a better price, or I'll call the cops on your ass myself."

Kira piped up, "Look, I don't have time to haggle. I'll give you two."

"Fine," Sid relented.

"And you'll throw that in case behind you." Kira completed the negotiation.

Sid glared at Kira and then his cousin. "TJ, the next time you plan on robbing me, bring your own gun."

The sight of the hundreds, Kira was pulling out of her shoulder bag changed Sid's attitude. His face split into a lop-sided smile, exposing a mouth wrecked by meth.

"I'll keep that in mind, tell your mom and dad hey for me."

"Yeah, sure, and don't forget the reunion is this Sunday," Sid reminded his cousin.

"I know, I'm bringing the hamburger patties."

Safonovo, Russia

The NATO column rumbled toward Moscow, unimpeded by the Russian military, which seemed atypical, although a few of the militia continued to harass the tanks, firing rocket propelled grenades at them, in an attempt to slow them down.

Ignoring the opposition, General Krol ordered his men to treat these Russians as little more than a picnic nuisance.

Rumbling into the town of Safonovo, Krol laughed when he saw a single Iskander-M blocking the M1 roadway.

"Pawel," he called down to his Weapons Operator. "Please remove that obstruction."

"Aye, General."

As Pawel sited the mobile weapons launcher, he saw the flare of the flames stream out of the end of the missile as it was discharged, bursting toward the atmosphere at Mach 6.

He fired a round into the launcher before it could rid itself of its second missile. The flash through the site blinded Pawel, momentarily.

The driver heard the General command him to rush through the burning wreckage before the first warhead fell back to Earth.

Opening the turbines to full speed, the lead tank demolished the flaming remains of the Russian vehicle, followed by a stream of tanks.

Suddenly, Krol heard the American Colonel in the rear yell into the radio, "Where the fuck did *that* launcher come—"

Two earth-shattering explosions shook the road beneath them. The radio crackled and squealed in Krol's ears, deafening him. He spun around in time to see twin mushroom clouds roll lazily skyward.

The first missile evaporated ten tanks in the middle of the column, mainly the Italian and Czech brigades, while the second… fired from a hidden launcher… annihilated the American 3rd Army tanks covering the rear.

Krol estimated them be one-kilo warheads, no doubt Russian President Kirill Golubev making good on his threat.

"If there are any tanks who can still hear me, do not stop or else you will suffer a worse fate than your comrades."

Washington, D.C.

The satellite radio music blaring through TJ's car speakers was giving Kira a migraine.

The driving bass and thumping drums were bad enough, made worse by lyrics which should never have seen the light of day, let alone screeched through loudspeakers.

Right now, two ice picks would come in very handy, so she could jam them in both ears to shut out the appalling racket.

To her relief, the wail of the *Emergency Alert System* interrupted the broadcast. Once the warning died down, an automated voice announced, "This is not a test. Please, remain tuned in for a live message from the President of the United States.

TJ complained, "That damn old fart ruins everything."

"Pull over," Kira ordered.

"You're the boss," TJ chortled, driving into the parking lot of a fast food restaurant.

"Now, shut up and listen."

The silence was broken by President Hyden's voice, "My fellow Americans, at four-thirty P.M., Moscow time, two tactical nuclear missiles were fired, prior to Russian President Golubev's deadline.

"Approximately eighty brave men and women from our coalition forces were killed in the blasts, including at least twenty American personnel stationed in Poland.

"I have spoken to President Golubev as well as the heads of the NATO nations to negotiate a ceasefire to prevent another travesty from occurring.

"As is the tradition of this great country, we seek a

peaceful solution. Like the sagacious path President James Earl Carter chose during the Iranian Hostage Crisis, I will discontinue my campaign until this matter is resolved.

"It would be negligent and heartless of me to put myself above those who perished in the name of justice.

"The prayers of myself and my family go out to the loved ones of those brave service members, and we shall ensure their lives were not taken in vain."

There was an overly dramatic pause, as though Hyden had more unwelcome news, he preferred not to deliver but, with a small sigh, forged ahead.

Hyden's first volley was aimed at the Reagan Conservatives, who blamed his ineffective immigration policies for America's current violence and economic woes.

"In light of world events, I am compelled to enact measures to safeguard our homeland. Until further notice, all immigration both legal and otherwise is suspended, and all persons currently in the custody of the Immigration and Customs Enforcement will be returned to their countries of origin.

"Unfortunately, we cannot risk allowing every Tom, Dick, and Hernández…" a clear shot at his VP, "…to cross the border freely.

"Anyone caught smuggling immigrants into the country, will be considered enemies of the United States, and dealt with under the strictest penalties available."

His next shot was aimed at the other end of the spectrum, the Obama Liberals.

"Furthermore, as Americans, I beg you to practice restraint and not see this as a reason to hoard gas and other essentials.

"Rest assured, the shelves in your local supermarkets will remain stocked and, to protect those caught at the bottom of the wage scale," Hyden knew not to call the vast constituency of the Democratic Party, poor, "the prices will be frozen within acceptable levels. Price gouging will not be tolerated by my administration.

"This also applies to the country's petroleum, fuel oil, and natural gas supplies. Arrangements have been made to tap into the emergency reserves and reopen drilling on federal lands, for the foreseeable future."

Next came Hyden's coup de grâce. He appeased the Sierra Club, the largest the conservationist association in the US, and with whom he had battled frequently.

"To the environmental organizations and naturalist clubs who work diligently to preserve those lands and the wildlife who populate the same, I ask for your help to ascertain all drilling is done in an ethical and safe manner.

"Thank you for your attention. May God bless us all."

The radio reverted to the annoying music without skipping a beat.

Impressive, Kira mused. *He literally kissed every American's ass.*

She said to TJ, "Hurry up and get us to the Library."

"Aye, Aye, mon capitaine."

While TJ found a parking space in the farthest corner of the structure — as instructed by Kira, who extracted his promise to keep the volume of his music down — she had made it through the front doors of the Library of Congress, set up her laptop on one of the beautifully ornate desks, and was seeing early Democratic presidential candidates polling numbers coming in.

Hyden had gained yet another boost in the rankings following his announcement.

While the man had yet to set foot in New Hampshire, he

had enough state representatives on the ground there, campaigning as his proxies. It was paying off.

He had a lead on Stefi, within the margin of error; her easy primary win for nomination, evaporating like the dawn's mist. Endorsements which should have been hers, were transferred to Hyden for his political and diplomatic prowess.

Triggering her VPN firewall, Kira used her third burner phone from behind it. The call pinged off a multitude of cell towers, in and out of the US.

Even with that convoluted transmission, it would take approximately two minutes for the NSA to track her down.

The number she called also belonged to a burner phone, but how secure *that* one was, Kira did not know.

Voicemail, rather than the person to whom she hoped to speak, answered, "You have reached…"

Impatiently, Kira waited for the directive, "…please leave your message after the tone. *Beep*."

"Gwen, it's Racine. Call me when you get this on…"

Against her better judgment, she left the number of the burner phone. It was imperative Stefi and Cisco were told their personal phones were being monitored by the government.

Beyond that, Kira wanted to check her friend was okay and, more importantly, to hear a, hopefully, friendly voice.

When she did not hear back from the candidate, immediately, Kira tried again. This time, the phone did not go to voicemail.

"I don't care what the polls say," the voice on the other end of the call shouted at an unseen aid in the background. "I'm neither conceding the race nor running as a third party. It's a couple of goddamned polls. Besides, this is America, everybody knows third party candidates never get elected President."

Attention turned to the caller, "Hello? And you better have a good explanation as to how you got this—"

"Christ, Gwen…"

That was enough to silence the Vice President of the United States.

"…I have exactly one minute and twenty seconds, thanks to you. Your old man is listening in on your calls and, whoever your friend is at National Steel Amalgamated," Kira hoped Stefi was smart enough to know she meant the NSA, "their inside information on your investment was not worth crap."

"Tell ya what, Racine," that let Kira know Stefi understood the context of the call. "We'll have coffee and catch up when I get home. Same place as usual?"

"Sure, 'cept you're not sticking me with the bill this time."

At the click of the call being disconnected, Kira destroyed the third burner phone and sim card.

After what seemed like forever, although it was only about an hour, the thumb drives were uploaded onto her computer. Kira stuffed everything into her satchel, and returned at a rapid clip to where, she hoped, TJ was waiting.

Barely halfway across the parking her ears were assaulted by the discordant blare of TJ's damn music reverberating around the concrete structure, the pillars acting as sound boards.

Increasing her pace, Kira yanked open the passenger door to be punched in the face by the din, which rattled her teeth.

Kira switched off the satellite radio, hollering, "TJ! What part of *Be Inconspicuous* did you not understand?"

"Whoa, girl, keep it down. Are you trying to get caught by the cops?"

"I should be asking you the same question." Kira grumbled, climbing into the car. "Ugh, just take me…"

That's when it hit her. She had nowhere to go, at least, not until Stefi got back.

"By the pissy look on your face, I take it you have nowhere to hide out. Unless you want to crash in some roach-infested hotel, may I make a suggestion?"

Kira blew a despondent sigh, "Why not. I'm out of ideas."

"Might I offer you sanctuary at my place? I don't think many of your people are gonna think to look in Anacostia for a panties-bunched white girl."

"Please, elaborate." Kira pinned TJ with a suspicious gaze.

"Nothing sketchy… sheesh, can't a guy offer a woman a room without her assuming it's sex?"

The irony in TJ's tone along with his dramatic eye roll, made Kira snort.

"Well, what's a girl to think?" she shot back.

"How about saying thank you to my purely altruistic generosity," he countered loftily, then confessed, cheeks reddening slightly, "I live with my parents, no hanky-panky under their roof."

"Do you even know what altruistic means," Kira taunted, then held up her palms at his mock outraged expression.

"Sorry. Thank you for your generosity, TJ. I should be honored to take you up on your kind offer," she accepted with a wry grin.

CHAPTER SEVENTEEN

It was late by the time they reached Anacostia. Weaving through streets lined with a blend of older, detached homes and rowhouses, TJ drew up in front of a freshly painted residence, nestled alongside one church, and across the street from another.

Kira checked them out as she alighted from the Oldsmobile. The church adjacent to the house looked as though it had started life as a fire station, whereas the one opposite fitted the image of a small neighborhood church.

Knowing she was overstepping by prying into TJ's private life, she asked, "So which one do you attend?"

"Neither," he said with a shrug. "We go to the Baptist Church a couple of blocks away, but Mama always said the closer to the Good Lord the better. Never thought she actually meant physically but, I guess, she likes hedging her bets."

TJ led Kira around the back of the house, rather than through the front door and into the parlor. His folks would be watching TV at this time of night, and he figured it would be easier to sneak in his guest via the kitchen than to confront his mom straight off the bat.

Things for TJ never went as planned.

He opened the back door, and came face to face with his mother.

"Boy, where the hell have you been? You missed supp—"

The older woman paused mid-sentence, staring over her son's shoulder at the white girl who was trying her best to become one with the air.

"Tidas Josiah Johnson…"

Despite fearing for her life at the hands of Mrs. Johnson, Kira could not stifle a chuckle, "Tidas?"

"Shut up," he muttered.

"Mister, explain what…" waving he hand over her son's shoulder, "What. Is. That?"

"Mama, stop freaking out."

"Watch your mouth, boy, and tell me why you are trying to sneak a girl into the house. You know the rules. That behavior is not tolerated in my house."

"Mrs. Johnson, if I may?" Kira stepped in to save TJ. "Your son has been a perfect gentleman today, chauffeuring me around DC. Unfortunately, I had a break-in at my apartment making it impossible to return home. He was offering me a place to stay until my friend—"

"Wait," Ma Johnson interrupted. "I know you. You're the crazy woman who's been all over the news."

Her gaze bore into her son, "TJ, what have you gotten yourself mixed up in. Get her out of my house this minute."

TJ raised his palms to stop his mother's rant. "What do you always preach about helping your neighbor? Don't make me cite James 2:14."

"Child, dontcha dare use the Good Book against me."

"'What good is it my brothers and sisters, if someone claims to have faith but has no deeds? Can such faith save them?'"

"Why is it you only remember scripture when it suits you," his mom retorted.

"Ya taught me well." He beamed innocently.

His answer elicited a side eye from the older woman, and the feigned threat of a backhand. Elbowing TJ aside, Mrs. Johnson shouted into the living room, "Elbert, get yourself upstairs and fix up the guest room. Looks like we have company."

While TJ's mom remained wary about having a wanted criminal in her house, once her son had explained the events of the afternoon, she was prepared to concede the Feds might be railroading the girl.

She even went as far as to cook a decent meal for Kira, saying, "You look like you could use some meat on those bones. Doesn't your mother feed you?"

"My mom lives in Berlin. I'm afraid, I don't see her very often."

"That's terrible, child. You should call her this minute and tell her you're being taken care of. I'm sure she is worried to death about you."

Kira smiled and promised to do so when this was all over.

"It's getting late, TJ," Mrs. Johnson observed. "Take Miss Monroe upstairs so she can get settled in."

"I appreciate the hospitality, ma'am." Kira rose from her chair. "I promise to be out of your hair first thing in the morning."

"I won't hear of it," the older woman objected. "I am well acquainted with the evil our government is responsible for. My grandparents marched from Selma to Montgomery with Dr. King, and faced down fire hoses in Birmingham. Now, get some sleep."

Not about to argue, Kira did as she was told.

Following TJ up the stairs, Kira made idle chit chat, "So Tidas, huh?"

"Don't start. Was supposed to be Midas James. My dad's a huge Michael Jordan fan, and figured, if I had the same initials, I'd somehow magically have his basketball skills.

"Somebody at the hospital made a typo, and bang, instead of Midas, I'm Tidas. My folks thought it was too complicated to change."

Reaching the top of the stairs, he faced Kira. "Happy now?"

She tapped her finger on her chin for a second. "I s'pose." Kira grinned, and tried to come up with a way to broach her next question without causing offense. In the end, blunt seemed easiest, "Um, do you have Wi-Fi?"

'Jesus—"

"I heard that, Tidas James," Mrs. Johnson exclaimed from the kitchen. "Don't use the Lord's name in vain."

Shaking his head, he muttered, "Damn woman has ears like a cat."

"I heard that, too," rang up the stairs.

"Anyway. *Yes,* we have Wi-Fi. We live in Anacostia, not an Afghan cave. Though I heard they get good reception there as well."

"Mind if I get the password?"

"Gonna cost ya."

"I'm sure it is."

Kira took advantage of the generosity extended by TJ and his family, staying for the next three days. She paid two hundred a night, well in excess of the amount TJ had suggested for the privilege because it came with three square meals, each plate laden with more food than any human could eat.

Mrs. Johnson ensured Kira was not disturbed while she worked. The peace and quiet allowed the latter's story to come together while in hiding.

When Thursday dawned, Kira sent emails to the major networks, offering each an exclusive on the story of government kidnapping, extortion, and, arguably, the sacrifice of NATO troops, all in the name of a presidential campaign.

With the exception of a fringe, ultraconservative network called *The American Truth News*, not a single one responded. The *ATN* only wanted the story if she was prepared to slant her report, to claim Hyden had ordered the attack directly. They did not care whether he had, for her to specify it in her account was sufficient for their purposes.

As tempting as this might be, Kira had no physical proof. Sullivan and those around Hyden would ensure any document containing information which could be construed as evidence never saw the light of day.

Realizing, by tendering the story, she had put the family at risk, Kira deemed it time to leave the Johnson's home.

Mrs. Johnson tried to reassure their guest that everything was okay, and begged her to stay a few more days. She was in full match-making mode, attempting to marry off her son to Kira.

As politely as she could, Kira declined the offer, softening her refusal by affirming that when it was safer, she would return for Sunday dinner with the family.

Mrs. Johnson made her promise.

After bidding her kindly hosts goodbye, Kira asked TJ to

drive her to one more location. The movie theater at the Reston Town Center.

By the time her chauffeur had finished demonstrating his James Bond driving skills through the side roads of DC, Kira was ten minutes late and the movie had already started.

She wasted valuable time wandering up and down the darkened aisles of the theater searching for her companion.

In the very front row, she saw the big floppy hat she had brought for Stefi at the Chincoteague Pony Swim the previous year. Kira chuckled at how much it blocked the screen for anyone sitting behind.

Although the theater was reasonably crowded, for a zombie apocalypse movie, Kira spied the empty seat next to Stefi, and dropped into it.

A bucket of popcorn, tossed through with the customary oily butter and chocolate candies, hit Kira in the chest.

"You're late, as usual," Stefi sniped, grabbing a handful. "Mind, I'd be amazed if you were early to anything."

"*Shhhhhhhhhhhh.*" The woman in the row behind Stefi demanded.

"Oh, shush yourself, puta," Stefi grumbled back.

"Wow, not very politically correct, there," Kira taunted.

"Shush to you, too. You know I hate these movies."

"Then why did you sit in the front row of all places?"

"Cuz, it wouldn't look good for the President—"

"*Vice* President," Kira corrected.

"*Future* President to be seen in the back row of a movie theater, especially with the likes of you. Why in the hell did you try to shoot your editor."

On the big screen, a group of zombies demolished a campsite, prompting the campers to retaliate.

"I wasn't seriously going to shoot Walter. We were having a disagreement on Property and Intellectual Property Rights, and I needed him to see it my way."

"Well, Calamity Jane, somebody did a good job of editing the video, because that's not what the expression on your face said."

As a zombie tore a leg from the body of a struggling girl, Stefi suggested, "How about we go to the bakery down the street? I can stomach it better than this."

"Shhhhhh," the woman repeated, earning herself a blizzard of popcorn and candy in her lap.

"Well, I nev—" the DC yuppie began.

Cutting her off, Stefi said, "Well, that explains a lot." Then in her best Haverstraw, New York Latina accent, drawled, "Hey, la perra, spoiler alert, they all get ate at the end."

Flipping off the annoying movie goer, Stefi marched out of the theater.

Kira watched her friend stomp down the aisle, shrugged at the woman, and ran after Stefi.

Once the two had settled at a small table with their coffee and scones, Kira filled Stefi in on everything she had missed while campaigning in New Hampshire.

Still wearing her hat, now accompanied by a pair of oversized sunglasses, creating the impression she was a deranged tourist, Stefi observed, "You're fucked, chica."

"Yeah, Sullivan did a good job of making me look insane."

"Can't blame him for that. You went above and beyond all by yourself."

"You started it."

Ignoring her friend, Stefi asked, "So now what?"

"I have a story everyone is afraid to touch, *and* I'm out of a job. Can I crash on your couch for a couple of days?"

"Not hardly, after your little stunt with Cisco's abuela, I can't trust anybody here in DC, and I'm not going to let you endanger my parents. Best I can do is smuggle you to my aunt's place in Puerto Rico."

"Won't that put her in danger?"

"I don't like her much, so I see no problem."

"Well, I do. I doubt the FBI is going to let me board a 787 and fly off to destinations unknown."

"Who says you're flying commercial?"

"Well, you sure can't transport me on Air Force Two. Hell, not even you can use it for campaign purposes."

"No law about me paying for a private jet, out of my own pocket, and traveling to San Juan to check on the damage done by this year's hurricanes. The Puerto Rican primaries are coming up in March."

"Won't the press attack you for your frivolous squandering of government funds?"

"Like they don't already? All I need to do is show, I paid for the flight out of personal funds, ain't nothing anybody can squawk at. By the way, how would you look in a flight attendant's uniform, and maybe blonde hair?"

Instinctively, Kira touched her signature black hair, a genetic trait passed down through the Monroe line. She had never thought of dying it.

A frown marred her face.

"Don't give me that look. I need you to look like a stewardess and not… like… well… you."

"You just want to see me in something sexy," Kira bantered, trying to make light of the situation.

"Oh, for Chrissakes," the VP growled. "Pay the bill and let's get out of here."

As the duo exited the café onto the sunny sidewalk full of shops, Kira ventured, "What am I supposed to do in San Juan?"

"Simple, chica. Write your story."

"For whom? If none of the networks will touch it, what makes you think a publisher will?"

Stefi stopped in her tracks to pin Kira with an incredulous look.

"Do you honestly think any publisher is *not* going to jump at the chance to publish a schlock story? Especially one from a famous journalist on the eve of Super Tuesday, with a forward by the Vice President of the United States?"

"Wait. You're giving me three months to write and edit this story?"

"What else are you planning to do in San Juan at this time of year? Too cold for lazing on the beach or swimming. If you're done with the questions, let's see what we can do with that hair of yours."

CHAPTER EIGHTEEN

Forty thousand feet over the Atlantic Ocean, heading to San Juan, Puerto Rico, the newest flight attendant, her blonde hair twisted into a French Pleat was in the rear of the plane being lectured in a hushed, angry tone by the purser.

"I don't know how you managed to get crewed onto this flight, but it is blindingly obvious, you have zero experience as a flight attendant.

"Explain to me how the fuck you managed to spill a tray full of martinis on that woman, and don't dare use turbulence as an excuse because we both know there wasn't any. While we're at it, do you have any idea who the hell you dumped those drinks on?"

"I'm guessing somebody who doesn't like olives?" Kira replied pertly.

"She's the goddamned Vice President of the United States."

"Hmm, can't say I recognized her. Besides, I voted for the other guy."

The purser hissed, "You had better straighten up."

The conversation came to an abrupt end when Vice President Hernández stepped out of the private lounge on the other side of the bulkhead.

Smoothing out any wrinkles as best as she could, Stefi gave Kira the stink-eye for the *accidental* martini bath.

The purser judged this an appropriate time to extricate herself from the situation. While she had performed her duties as professionally as possible, she assumed the VP would finish excoriating the clumsy flight attendant.

Once the two were alone, an in as contrite a tone as she could summon — considering she blamed Stefi for forcing her to dye her hair, turning her into a red carpet, bleached blonde — Kira apologized again, so the rest of the passengers could hear, "I am so sorry, ma'am. Would you like a fresh drink?"

"No thank you. I've worn enough for this flight."

"Would you like me to serve you dinner?"

"What are we having?"

"Spaghetti…with ragu…"

Stefi looked down at her fresh, white blouse. Horrifying images of her looking like an extra in a gangster movie raced through her head, as Kira finished the description.

"…and meatballs. Lovely chunky ones."

"Is there another choice?"

"Clams in cream sauce."

"I'll have that instead," Stefi said.

"Very well, ma'am," Kira replied. "Would you like red wine with that?"

As Stefi began to make her way back to her seat, Kira's question stopped her in her tracks.

Pivoting slowly, she leaned closer to the *flight attendant,* and said in a voice only the two could hear, "If *one* drop of dinner finds its way to my top, I will personally toss you out the door and into the ocean."

Then, Stefi flashed Kira a smile, leaving the latter to wonder whether the she was serious.

San Juan, Puerto Rico

The remainder of the flight to Luis Muñoz Marín International Airport was incident free. The jet touched down and taxied to a military hangar, where four of the five passengers, along with three of the four crew members made their way down the mobile stairway to the vehicles below whose engines were already idling.

These people departed in a black Tahoe, en route to the main terminal. They had been ordered to remain on standby until the Vice President was ready to depart, which meant no relaxing with a drink in the bar.

The other vehicle, a military-grade Hummer with darkened windows, waited for the last two to descend from the jet.

On the heels of the Vice President, came a black suited, female Secret Service agent with a government-standard, blonde ponytail; eyes hidden behind aviator sunglasses, fingers pressed to her ear as though speaking to someone.

"The Football is hiked and in play. The Football is being lateraled to the chariot. The Football has crossed the goal line."

"Why do I put up with you?" Stefi asked in exasperation as the two settled into the vehicle.

"Cuz I entertain you," *Agent* Kira replied.

Aware her friend watched way too many spy thrillers, Stefi did see fit to correct Kira on one rather salient point. "You understand when the Secret Service refers to the Football, they're talking about the launch codes for the nukes."

"And here I thought they were talking about Hyden's gambling debts. Go figure." Kira grinned. "You have to admit, I'd make a great Secret Service agent?"

"If you ever drew that stupid gun to protect me, I'm sure you would shoot me in the foot, and then yourself. Surprised you didn't wing Walter when you aimed it at him."

Kira stuck out her tongue. "When are you going to forget that little incident? A whole lot of fuss over nothing. In any case, remind me to push you in front of me if anyone starts shooting. From what I see in the voters' polls, you could use the bump in your ratings for heroism."

"And that's the Kira, I love."

The Hummer exited the hangar and drove out of the airport onto Expreso 26.

The route skirted the outer edge of San Juan, but when they turned onto Autop. José de Diego, Expreso 22, a puzzled Kira observed to the driver, "Excuse me, sir, surely if you understand Spanish, you must realize San Juan is that way." Pointing at the conurbation to their left.

The stern-faced Marine did not respond. His attention fixed on the vehicle ahead, another Hummer. It had taken the lead of the cavalcade of matching vehicles which had fallen in line behind.

Kira felt a nervous twinge ping the pit of her stomach as the Vice President's ride was surrounded.

Stefi took no notice, informing Kira, matter-of-factly, "Change of plans, chica. Seems my aunt did not want the company of a gun-toting, white girl from the mainland.

"Plan B is to take you to my parents' beach bungalow in Isabela. You'll have the house and the beach to yourself. Whatever you do, *Do Not* get murdered there or they will hire some Haitian mambo to resurrect you, so they can kill you themselves."

Kira saluted the VP. "Aye, aye, Chief. No blood to be spilled on the teak floors."

"Please, Kira, take this seriously. We both are walking a thin line."

"I'm sorry, Stefi. I'm just trying not to go crazy with everything that's going on."

"Then alone time on the beach is just what you need."

The parade turned down a long drive to a property set away from any neighbors, and surrounded by a substantial, and very high, stone wall.

A pair of beautiful but solid, Scandinavian redwood gates — stained to accent the wood's natural character and protect it from the elements — operated by an automatic opener, prevented unauthorized access.

The entourage remained outside the gates, which swung open soundlessly, while the Hummer transporting Kira and Stefi carried on, coming to a halt on the circular frontage, alongside an imposing set of double doors, carved from the same timber as the gates, which towered over the pair.

Kira stared, agog.

Stefi ushered her in, acting as though the place was anything but spectacular.

Inside, Kira discovered the house was automated, including the security system which monitored every corner of the property.

Sporting numerous spacious bedrooms and bathrooms, it was obvious the house was built to accommodate Stefi's large extended family.

Through the back door, off the chef's kitchen, Kira's gaze travelled beyond the hot tub, and blue-tiled pool, to a secluded, fenced off beach, and the vast expanse of the Atlantic Ocean.

After the impromptu tour, Kira asked, "Is your family into drug smuggling?"

Stefi chuckled. "White slavery, actually. Why do you think you're here alone?"

"Haha, very funny... *not*."

"On that note, I will bid you adieu."

"What? You're not even going to stay to cook me dinner?"

"Not hardly. I have a Presidency to win. Now you're out of my hair, I have a fighting chance."

A quick hug and Stefi was gone.

Kira ran to the security room, and pressed buttons like a child with a Christmas toy. She happened across the camera aimed at the road leading away from the house, and watched the parade of SUVs re-organize their line-up, as the Vice President of the United States prepared to return to San Juan.

When the last Hummer disappeared out of sight, Kira was swamped by a wave of loneliness. Although she had spent the majority of her adult life without company, this was true isolation... a prisoner of Devil's Island... without the leprosy.

Raiding the fully stocked refrigerator, in which she found a veritable smorgasbord of meats and cheeses, Kira was relieved to see her friend had not left her to starve to death.

Curling up on the couch to watch the news on the seventy-two inch, flat screen television, Kira nibbled the food, while listening to the newscaster begin his spiel about the escalation of the war in Russia and Belarus.

The Ukrainian army's siege of Minsk, persists, as do the demands for the unconditional surrender of Belarus President for

Life, Igor Trubila. Reports from within the city contend that the food shortages, and disruptions to electricity and water, hark back to the privations suffered during the Second World War.

While early snow and staunch resistance from the Russians, who have begun conscripting men from the far east of the country, have prevented the Polish-led NATO forces from advancing into Moscow, the volley of rocket barrages between the two forces continues unabated, despite President Hyden brokering a cease-fire.

Following the use of nuclear weapons, which claimed the lives of American soldiers from the Third Army, Hyden has refused to risk further losses, demanding multilateral talks in a bid to end hostilities.

In other news...

Kira had heard enough. Going to her bedroom, she retrieved her laptop, and headed to the back patio.

The sun was setting, but the evening breeze from the Atlantic held a reminder of the day's heat. Drawing a breath of the balmy night air, she began writing...

The Lesser of Two Evils

...and did not stop until the first rays of dawn broke over the horizon.

CHAPTER NINETEEN

The first two months of the Democratic caucuses and primaries behind them, Hernández and Hyden found themselves in a race not seen since the 2008 primaries, when an unknown Barack Obama came out of obscurity to defeat Hillary Clinton — until then, the party's favorite.

New Hampshire favored the incumbent for re-election, while South Carolina and Nevada went to his Vice President.

The Sunday before the state's February 29th primary, the pair was in Michigan, vying for the Great Lakes State's one hundred and forty convention delegates, running neck and neck.

Hyden had attempted to bribe the United Auto Workers to support him by re-opening plants abandoned by the auto manufacturers when they moved to China and Mexico. Hyden's plan was to use these factories, and the UAW workers, displaced in the relocations, to produce a new era of *Peace Through Strength*.

As for the European dilemma, the situation had ground to a stalemate in Belarus. Both sides were scraping through the snow for food and water.

Years of warfare with Russia had left Ukraine with next to no surplus rations to support an extended siege of Belarus, and they refused to negotiate a permanent cease-fire, determined to punish their neighbors for allowing the Russians to use their lands as a gateway to attack Kyiv.

The residents stranded in Minsk were reportedly descending into cannibalism because their *esteemed* leader — living in the lap of luxury, secure in his mansion, under highly armed and well-fed guards — refused to capitulate.

The Poles had broken through the Russian defenses and breached Moscow, to find it in the same condition as did Napoleon, two and a half centuries earlier... deserted.

It was a hollow victory for General Krol, especially after losing the bulk of his forces, and being abandoned by the Americans.

He and his men were stranded in the empty city, unable to return to Warsaw through the radioactively contaminated deadman's land which lay between them and the Belarus border.

Isabela, Puerto Rico

Thousands of miles away, the newest resident of Isabela, Puerto Rico, enjoyed the tranquility of her hideaway, secure from the meltdown occurring across the ocean.

On tenterhooks for two weeks waiting for her publisher, Dermot Quantrill, to contact her regarding the release of her book, Kira decided a distraction was in order.

She wandered around the local market in search of ingredients for dinner, and followed that up with an afternoon lazing on the beach.

To relax was not in Kira's nature but, right now, there was little else to do.

Kira walked up the beach after a dip in the warm salty water. Wrapping herself in a towel and wringing out her hair, she noticed a missed call on her cell.

Scooping up her phone, she saw it was from Quantrill.

"Typical," Kira muttered.

She pressed redial and, in a cheery voice, greeted, "Mr. Quantrill, how may I be of service?"

"Where the hell are you? I need you in DC a-sap. Your book is exploding all over the networks."

"Wait… what? I didn't think it was released yet."

"It isn't, but somehow, someone from CNN got an advanced copy, and decided to post some derogatory comments. You wouldn't happen to have any idea how they managed that, do you?"

"N-No, sir," Kira stammered a reassurance, although she had a pretty good idea who was behind the leak. She had sent out only one other copy, but she would deal with that later.

"Anyway, suddenly you're on the Best Seller lists for pre-orders on multiple platforms. Hyden's polling numbers took a broadside because of your accusations, leaving Hernández to take Michigan along with a substantial lead in the delegate count.

"I want you on all the networks tomorrow to defend your book, and see to it the Vice President succeeds."

"That's going to be easier said than done, sir. Stef- I mean the Vice President helped smuggle me out of the country to a safe haven. I can't very well ask her to drop everything to fly me back."

"Look, Miss Monroe, I don't care how you get to DC, just get there. The publishing company will cover the cost—"

"That is generous of you," Kira thanked him.

"Out of your advance, of course," Quantrill added.

"Of course," Kira's sarcasm was lost on the publisher. "Why would anyone think differently?"

"I'll have a car meet you at Dulles Airport tonight at eight. Make sure you're there."

Looking at the clock, Kira realized it was already two, and the flight took three hours. Biting her tongue, she countered, "This advance had better be outstanding."

The next call Kira made was to Stefi. At this point, hiding from the Feds was no longer plausible, and the VP was the only one who could possibly accommodate her request.

A tired voice answered on the other end, "Let me guess, you set the bungalow on fire."

"Very funny," Kira chided. "It's not anything so drastic. I just need a ride."

"Chica, in case you haven't been watching TV, I'm in Michigan. Can't really pick up your ass."

"I know that, silly. I just need you to send a helicopter."

"Oh, really. That's all, huh?"

"Well, that, and can you arrange for a private jet to get me home?"

"Are you insane, Kira?"

"You made me write this book, this is all on you."

Stefi huffed a harassed sigh, "And when do you need all of this transportation by?"

"Within the hour?"

The line went dead. Either Stefi was getting right on the arrangements, which Kira deluded herself into believing or, she was going to be left high and dry.

Either way, she scurried to the bedroom to pack.

Less than thirty minutes later, a Blackhawk Helicopter dropped onto the bungalow's drive to transfer Kira to the airport where the waiting jet took off, immediately Kira was on board.

Unlike the flight *to* Puerto Rico, this plane had no amenities. Basic was the best description, she could come up with, as the lone passenger on a Lockheed Martin C-5M Super Galaxy, transporting cargo to the States.

Her fold-down seat lacked any level of comfort, and the clear-air turbulence over the Bermuda Triangle left her certain the flight was destined to end up in a parallel dimension.

Landing at Joint Base Andrews, instead of Dulles, meant she missed the promised car, and had to fork out fifty-dollars for a cab ride to the city.

Washington, D.C.

A three AM call from the night porter of the first decent hotel, Kira had spotted on her ride from Andrews, jarred her awake. Disoriented, she tried to recall where she was and why the phone was ringing.

Grappling with the handset, she mumbled, "Hello?"

"This is the front desk, ma'am, with your wake up call. Your rental car is scheduled to arrive at 4:30."

For a sizable tip, the concierge was happy to oblige his guests' requests… no matter how outlandish. So, the request for a rental car to be at the front of the hotel was not out of the norm, though the insistence on it being a Highland Green 1968 Ford Mustang GT fastback, bordered on the absurd.

Nevertheless, money is money.

"Thank you," Kira blurted out and dropped the phone back on its cradle.

Showered and dressed, Kira made it downstairs in time to grab a cinnamon roll and coffee, before sliding into the leather driver's seat. Racing the engine for a moment, she shifted into first and burned the tires on her way out of the parking lot.

It's not every day you get to drive an iconic car, she justified her juvenile behaviour.

The first interview of the day was with a local network affiliate, one which favored the current President and not the Vice President.

Primped and primed by the station's hair and make-up team, Kira loitered in the wings to be seated for the interview. It was obvious the woman assigned the task had not seen an advanced copy of the book, because she was flipping through the list of questions the producers had, evidently, just given her to ask.

As the light on the camera flashed red, the woman became cool and collected.

"Welcome back, everyone."

Kira glanced at the clock on the wall. It was 5:30. Unlikely to be much of a viewing audience, except for vampires, and shady politicians sneaking into their houses after a night with their mistresses.

"Following the footsteps of her father and great grandfather, Kira Monroe of the famed Monroe family, has joined us this morning to talk about her new book, *The Lesser of Two Evils*.

"Ms. Monroe, why did you choose this particular title?"

"Well, Julia," Kira decided to kill the interviewer with

kindness. "If you ask the majority of Americans who they voted for and why, they will say they chose the lesser of two evils. Is that any way to determine who we want in the White House? Shouldn't the candidate be anything but evil?"

"Then, your critics' accusations are true. You wrote this tripe primarily as a hit piece on President Hyden?" No beating about the bush here, the woman went straight for Kira's jugular.

"If you mean, do I believe that, despite Hyden's assertion he is the *Candidate of Reason and Peace*, his hands are stained with the blood of innocent soldiers on both sides of the Russian conflict, then yes, I'm happy to see his polling has been affected because someone deemed it acceptable to leak a copy of my book to various news sources."

"Do you have any evidence to support your contention? I'm sure none in the White House will validate such wild allegations, except maybe your friend, and President Hyden's chief rival, Vice President Estefanía Hernández.

"*Our* sources, who agreed to speak to us on the grounds of anonymity, contest that the Vice President used campaign funds illegally, to fly you out of the country in October.

"Would you like to refute this claim?"

Kira did not take the bait. She knew this game well, it was one she played more than a few times.

Sitting back, she smiled. "I suggest you direct any questions concerning Vice President Hernández's spending to her campaign. She shares her abuela's Tembleque recipe with me, but not her financial statements."

Kira concluded the interview, her voice dripping saccharine sweetness, "While, I might have failed to increase your measly ratings, I assure you, *your* nonsense has pushed my sales even higher. Readers love a good scandal."

She unhooked her microphone and, before the woman

could come up with an adequate retort, Kira was off the stage and heading out of the station.

"I hope the network is smart enough to fire the bitch," she groused to the breaking dawn.

Kira climbed into the Mustang and turned on the ignition. As the muscle car leapt to life, she felt the cold, heavy metal edge of a gun barrel just behind her ear.

A voice from the backseat instructed, "Do not bother to look in the mirror, Ms. Monroe, I am confident you already know who I am, and please keep both hands on the steering wheel. It would be a shame to tarnish such a beautiful car… for the moment, at least."

"I'm honored to meet you in person, finally, Mr. Hutchinson. Should I bother asking why President Hyden's Chief of Staff is sitting in my backseat holding a gun to my head?"

"Let's just say I knew an invite to my office would cause Jamison more trouble than you're worth. If you don't mind, shift the car into gear, carefully."

"Where are you taking me?"

"Loudon County is pretty this time of year."

"Jesus Christ, can't you people choose somewhere closer when you kidnap me?"

Hutchinson tapped the barrel of the gun on Kira's skull. "Now, Now, Ms. Monroe, being testy isn't going to help. Drive."

Kira felt the pressure of the weapon lift as her passenger settled into his seat.

She judged she had time to concoct a plan to alter what they had in mind for her destiny. The weight of the Makarov in her coat pocket provided a semblance of security, but it was imperative she devised a way to extricate the pistol before Hutchinson pulled his trigger.

CHAPTER TWENTY

Virginia

Kira passed several Virginia state troopers as she drove west. Fearing for her life, the journalist in her refused to let this story die. If anyone held its conclusion, it would be Chief of Staff, Reginald Hutchinson.

Hutchinson had served as Hyden's financier during the President's time as a used car salesman. Hutchinson had sold Hyden on the premise that wealth was not made by selling overpriced vehicles, but by offering finance at exorbitant interest rates, then repossessing the vehicles the instant an installment was late.

As he had put it to Hyden, "It's not in the delivering of the item, it's giving Americans what they think they want but obviously can't afford."

From there, he became Hyden's campaign manager in his Florida State Representative and Federal Senate runs. He also facilitated Hyden's nomination for the number two spot on Rollins's ticket.

Whispers he was connected to foreign money, due to the depth of Hyden's war chest, followed Hutchinson but the accusations never gained traction.

As the cityscape transitioned into the horse pastures and dormant vineyards of Loudoun County, Kira found herself on the Greenway heading toward Leesburg.

Thoughtfully, Hutchinson threw an Instant Pass device over the seat so Kira did not have to dig for money or speak to any of the toll guards.

"Do you mind telling me where we're going?"

"To an appropriate place where we can end the problems your ridiculous book has generated. Follow the signs to Ball's Bluff Battleground."

"Since it appears this is a one way trip for me, would you mind satisfying my journalistic curiosity?"

"You mean, why I'm willing to kill you for Jamison Hyden?"

"That'll do for starters."

"Isn't it obvious? I've invested too much in the man to let you ruin everything. President Hyden will go down in history as the man who saved the world from annihilation."

"By starting a nuclear war? Doesn't seem very altruistic on Hyden's part."

"As the Royalist counter-revolutionary, François de Charette, is alleged to have said when accused of being responsible for numerous deaths during the French Revolution, 'You can't make an omelet without breaking eggs.'"

"That's a very cavalier attitude when it comes to the murder of thousands in order to let your man keep a job for which he is unqualified."

"Talking about being cavalier, why on earth did you choose such an ostentatious rental car?"

"I knew one of you freaks would show up, just thought I'd

be helpful. To be honest, I hoped it would be Hyden's lapdog, Sullivan. It wouldn't be the first time, he had me kidnapped, and he knows how to show a woman a fun time."

"Sorry to disappoint you, my dear Ms. Monroe. Regrettably, our future Vice President has neither the time nor the guile to deal with the likes of you."

The entrance to the battlefield loomed large in front of them.

"Once you enter the park, take the service road on the right."

"Is there any way I can persuade you to change your mind, and we part friends?"

"I doubt you and I could ever be friends, Ms. Monroe, and I don't relish the idea of finding my name in whatever rag you end up writing for… *if* you ever find another job. This way is better for both of us. Stop here."

"May I ask one last question?" Kira cruised slowly along the lonely service road.

"Never let it be said I'm not a gentleman. Ask."

"Why would you risk getting caught murdering me? Why not just have one of your lackeys do it?"

"Because, Ms. Monroe, it was trusting others to carry out my instructions which caused this catastrophe in the first place. You know, if you want something done correctly and all."

Kira heard Hutchinson shift forward in his seat, and felt the barrel of the weapon against her head. It was now or never.

Ramming the accelerator to the floor, the Mustang shot forward, sending both occupants reeling backwards, except Kira was ready for it.

To keep Hutchinson off balance, she cranked the wheel to the right, and released her grip. As the car spun out of control, Hutchinson fired. The shot went wild, but still grazed Kira's shoulder as she dove for cover behind the front seat.

The pistol barely out of her coat pocket, she fired through the seat back, striking Hutchinson in the stomach. Two more shots followed in quick succession, hitting him in the chest, and the last burrowing into the backseat when he slumped over.

Peeking over the seat, Kira saw Hutchinson's gun on the floor, blood stains blossoming across his expensive dress shirt.

He tried to say something, but his lips twitched then drooped as the life in his eyes ebbed.

For a moment, Kira leaned against her seat and stared at him. She tried to construct what her next move might entail but, for now, it seemed the biggest threat in her life had been vanquished.

Washington, D.C.

When the news of Reginald Hutchinson's death hit the midday news, the White House had a cover statement prepared.

Press Secretary, Bill Foster, stood before the Press Corps, a hint of anger and betrayal in his voice.

"Ladies and Gentlemen, it's my unfortunate duty to confirm the demise of the Presidential Chief of Staff, Reginald Hutchinson."

While the precise circumstances surrounding Hutchinson's death were yet to be established, the Communications Office had whipped up an announcement for the Press Security to practice until he hit every inflection perfectly.

"We do not have all the details regarding Hutchinson's death, but we do know he, along with the Joint Chiefs of Staff, had colluded to stage an overthrow of Russian President Kirill Golubev, by providing misleading information to President Hyden.

"As we speak, President Hyden has negotiated a permanent ceasefire between Russia and NATO…"

What Foster did *not* divulge was the two hundred billion euros, Hyden had sent to the Russians and the Poles. It was amazing how much peace could be purchased at America's expense.

"…In addition to Polish troops being airlifted from Moscow, ceding control of the city to its rightful governance, the troops from Ukraine have lifted their siege of Minsk and returned to their home country.

"United Nations troops will be stationed between Belarus and Ukraine to ensure the peaceful transition of leadership following the reported deaths of President for Life, Igor Trubila, and his family at the hands of the residents of the city.

"We will not be taking any questions because, at this time, we have no answers. Thank you and good afternoon."

Questions were yelled at Foster as he left the podium. True to his word, he answered none of them and exited the room.

The war behind him, Hyden was no longer a prisoner of the White House. Unable to avoid a Michigan loss, his strong showing during the Super Tuesday Primaries the following week, kept him in the running against his current Vice President.

Even as the final ballots were being counted in the June

primaries of New Jersey, South Dakota, Montana, and New Mexico — states whose primaries had not mattered in the past — the two were in a deadlock. Thanks, in part, to the emergence of a third candidate, a Silicon Valley Industrialist who had managed to garner delegates in the latter part of the campaign.

Hyden was rescued from the disaster of a possible coup within his cabinet by the arrest, removal, subsequent prosecution and courts martial of the Joint Chiefs for their participation.

Once more, the terms of punishment were never released to the public. In exchange for agreeing to fall on their swords — although disgraced — they were permitted to retire on full pension; and not at their lower grades, despite having lost the equivalent of two stars each.

In the wake of Hutchinson's death, Hyden ran as the politician of Peace. The recent conflict had demonstrated nuclear weapons were unusable in any context, be it tactical or strategic, and the only difference between the two was the number of lives lost, and the amount of land blighted for generations.

Much to the chagrin of the military industrial complex, Hyden began campaigning on the platform that conventional weapons needed to be scaled back.

Booed by veterans groups, the younger voters cheered him on. It did not matter where his votes came from, he welcomed them all.

In a bold move, when the convention opened in Los Angeles, Hyden pushed to be granted the opening keynote address, instead of the planned speech from former President Gwyneth Rollins.

He wanted to step out of her shadow and into the limelight.

It was an opportunity to strike while the iron was hot, in hopes of sewing up the nomination, no later than the second convention vote. He feared subsequent rounds of voting would strengthen the chances of that treacherous bitch stealing *his* nomination.

Security was tight in the Los Angeles Convention Center, as well as the bleed over in the Arena next door. To blend in with the crowds, members of the FBI and the Security Services were attired as delegates and revelers.

Up in the catwalks, snipers were positioned in case anyone tried to charge the podium during the speeches. These men were dressed in black, so no one below would notice them.

Cheers and music blared throughout the complex when President Jamison Hyden took the stage. A gasp echoed through those assembled, followed by a stunned hush.

The attendees were expecting to see the former President or, at least, her First Lady to give the opening address, echoing a similar performance by the Obamas at the same convention nearly two decades earlier.

Chuckling inwardly at the sea of confused faces, Hyden started his speech. "This reminds me of the convention twelve years ago in Philadelphia, when the charming and savvy Gwyneth Rollins announced me as her running mate to an equally stupefied audience.

"Over the next three terms, as both her Vice President and your President, her choice proved to be wise and, I stand before you one last time, to ask you to put your faith in me as she did so many years ago."

Applause reverberated around the hall; half in support of the President and half due to the fact, they were on live television. To present anything less than a unified front gave the Republicans more fodder against the Democrats in November.

Hyden resumed his speech before anyone could intervene.

"As a country, we have had our fill of successes and hardships, these last three terms…" a not very subtle attempt to blame his blunders on decisions made by his predecessor, "…but through it all, we have persevered."

Obligatory applause.

Hyden lifted his palms for silence, like a conductor leading the brass section.

"Even the recent hostilities in Europe, demonstrated that America remains the leader of the free world and, despite those who work against us, we shall triumph and endure."

This brought thunderous applause.

Hyden stretched his arms above his head, his fingers extended in "V for Victory" signs, reminiscent of Richard Nixon during the Vietnam War.

He began to deliver his proposed platform for a fourth and final term. One based on chopping off the legs of the military by their collective knees, for the betterment of the general population.

A shot rang out.

No one knew where it came from.

The high powered projectile struck Hyden in the chest and he dropped like a stone. Security drew their weapons and surrounded the fallen President as medical staff rushed forward.

A scuffle in the far side catwalk, wrested everyone's attention to the rear of the convention center. Guns rattled, and a body plummeted to the floor, taking out a number of chairs.

Screams erupted and people charged for the doors. Those not fast enough to avoid the stampede were crushed to death under foot.

Including the President and the supposed assassin, eleven people died in the chaos.

Kira Monroe watched the melee unfolding at the Democratic Convention on the television in her Washington hotel room. The two guards stationed in the corridor outside her door, made it impossible for her to leave.

She had no idea *who* was responsible for that.

As the hours ticked by, information filtered through naming Gunnery Sergeant Pritchard Johnson as the shooter. Johnson, stationed at Camp Lejeune was reported AWOL a month ago, around the same time as whispers he was connected to Corporal John Wayne Davis's death began to emerge.

Whispers, Kira had been tracking with avid interest.

She ears pricked up. She *knew* Davis had not acted alone, but until now his co-conspirator had remained a ghost... the irony of that not lost on her. Her theory proven, she allowed herself a smug smile.

Wonder what prompted him to shoot Hyden though, she ruminated. A question Kira acknowledged might never be answered, however much that frustrated her. One more thread she could not tie off.

Until the next morning.

As Kira was deleting the usual collection of trivia, her mouse paused at an email from someone whose address started *Gjohnsonpd.* She frowned, and the hairs went up on the back of her neck.

No freakin' way.

Given her relationship with the various branches of American security, Kira maintained the highest level of protection available on her laptop. How did this get through her firewalls? Was it a phishing attempt, or someone trying to plant malware?

She clicked on the sender's address… no weird suffixes. Didn't mean a virus wasn't embedded somehow. Raising all the shields on her computer, she took a risk.

Her jaw dropped.

It was a confession, of sorts, detailing the circumstances surrounding the attack on the village in Poland. Names — from the pilot who flew Johnson and Davis to Vilnius, to the top brass who ordered the operation — were dropped. Specifics, known only to those involved were scattered through the rather meandering narrative.

By the time she reached the last line, Kira had no doubt Johnson fired the rockets which destroyed a village, killing hundreds of innocent civilians, and triggering a conflict which had catapulted the world to the brink of annihilation.

It was difficult to tell whether Gunnery Sergeant Pritchard Johnson deemed the initial attack heinous, whether he was sorry for his part in it, or whether his explosive revelation was because, in the aftermath of the war, he was worried about his job.

How Johnson had obtained her contact information was a mystery, although Kira guessed someone at the publishing house had loose lips. That said, she wished she could thank him.

Now, she had her story!

Not to mention she could satisfy the curiosity of a certain Russian Minister of Foreign Affairs, Fyodor Mikhaylov. If she played her cards right, Kira reckoned she could wangle the promised dinner and drinks with the Minister *and* his wife.

That could wait.

She had an expose to write.

Crowing, "Oh, happy day," in, admittedly, unholy glee, Kira's fingers flew across the keyboard.

Truth will out.

Hyden's assassination effectively canceled the Democratic Convention. As with John F Kennedy, the world mourned for three days, buried him, and moved on.

The Democratic National Committee agreed to nominate Estefanía Hernández to run for President, which she won — easily.

Her election as America's fiftieth president, did not lead to demands for recounts or an international investigation. America was happy with its choice. When the political pundits polled people as to why they voted for Hernández, fewer than ten percent uttered the phrase, she was the Lesser of Two Evils.

The driving factor for her victory were the issues she advocated.

Kira — despite the deaths or subsequent arrests and prosecutions of those responsible for the *terror attack* on Poland — no longer felt safe in Washington, or anywhere else in the United States for that matter.

The move to Berlin to stay with her mother was no less challenging.

"Mom, are you sure the airport hasn't rung about my lost luggage?"

"No, kätzchen, for the last time, no one has called. Did you check *your* cell phone?"

"For Chrissakes, mom—"

"Kira Monroe, don't you dare take the Lord's name in vain."

"Since when did you find religion?"

"The Lutherans are famous for their potlucks. Who knows, might even find you a stepfather there."

"As if, and ewww." Kira shuddered.

Ding Dong

Mercifully, the chime of the doorbell ended further discussion about her mother's romantic adventures.

"Love…"

Kira was always at how smoothly her mother's terms of

endearment slipped from one language to another. *Result of all the countries, Dad dragged us to, I guess.*

"...could you see who's at the door?"

"Why me? It's your house."

"I'm busy here. Anyway, it could be a Lost Baggage clerk from Heathrow with your luggage."

"Very funny. I already told you, I didn't fly through London, so they wouldn't have my bags.

Kira marched to the door, throwing over her shoulder, "Honestly, I don't know whether you or Dad has the worst sense of humor."

"Well, since he's not here to defend himself, I'd say his was worse."

Facing the kitchen, her hand on the doorknob, Kira chided, "Great, now we'll have to suffer his ghost popping up to present the opposing..."

She turned to greet the visitor, her last word falling from suddenly frozen lips, "...view."

On the doorstep, attired in full Russian dress uniform, cap tucked smartly under his arm, stood Lieutenant Colonel Leonid Ilyich Gusev.

Kira's jaw dropped, as tears welled.

"Greetings, are you perchance, Ms Kira Monroe, world renowned writer and journalist?"

"I-Is it r-really you, Leo?" Kira stammered.

A smile brightened his face, "Da, I am he."

"I don't understand. I couldn't reach you, and Sullivan insinuated you were dead."

"As you can see, I am very much not a phantom." He chuckled.

"Why did you not contact me?"

"Russia's glorious President and his Cabinet felt we had

provided you with enough intel. Given your close connection to your current President — who, if I may say, is not open to foreign contributions, unlike her predecessor, making her impossible to control — left our government fearful of trusting you. We needed to let the dust settle. Please to be assured, *I* never doubted you."

"Enough, already," Kira commanded, "Just get in here."

"I am afraid not yet, Ms. Monroe. First, I have important business to complete for Mother Russia."

Reaching into his pocket, Leo pulled out a narrow official-looking black leather case.

Kira was baffled. *Jewelry, really Leo?*

Her flippant remark died in her throat when Leo opened the lid.

On a cushion of black velvet, two items glinted in the sunlight. A crest and a star.

Kira studied the crest. A crowned, double-headed eagle in delicate black enamel with gilt detail, bearing the blue St. Andrew's cross, complete with crucified saint embossed on it.

Engraved on the tip of each arm of the saltire, the Latin letters *SAPR* — St. Andrew, Patron of Russia.

Alongside, an eight-pointed silver star at the center of which, a miniature of the crest embedded in gold, encircled by a blue ring bearing the motto, *For Faith and Loyalty*, and encrusted with diamonds as a special distinction.

A historian, Kira did not need Leo to explain that she was looking at Russia's highest civilian medal, The Order of St. Andrew. The only thing she wanted to know was *why*?

"Explain yourself, Lieutenant Colonel Gusev."

"Yes, yes, perhaps a trifle extraordinary. I *did* try to convince the President you were more of a... what is that amusing colloquialism you were fond of, ah yes... beer and brats girl, but he insisted. This particular medal once belonged to Count Fyodor Golovin."

He twinkled down at Kira. His delight at being able to confer this unheard of honor on her, obvious.

"*Extraordinary?* Understatement of the decade. Hang on, wasn't Golovin the first person to be awarded the order by Peter the Great?"

"So I understand. Apparently, President Golubev knew of the fascination and appreciation you and your family have for history and, since you did save my country… more or less… he felt it appropriate to confer it onto you."

"Why is Golubev not here to present this trinket himself?"

"For some reason, the Germans and Poles are upset by the waste of military resources expended during their invasion of Russia. Can you believe how ludicrous that sounds? He surmised sending an envoy might go unnoticed. He did not elaborate on why *I* was his choice."

Stunned, Kira might be, but that did not stop her from making a crazy signature move. Instead of taking the medal, she snatched Leo's cap. It was against military protocol to do so, but she had seen it in a movie, and figured she would never get another chance.

Placing it on her head, backwards, she grinned impishly. "I think I might know the reason. Next time you speak to your President, please tell him, I am pleased with his other gift as well."

Stretching up on her tiptoes, she kissed him.

Leo reciprocated with devastating passion.

When Stefi asked for questions at her first news conference, after being sworn in as President — three months after her landslide victory — the quickest to rise was a woman at the back of the room.

Acknowledging the journalist — who had made a name for herself recently by risking life and limb to print the truth — Stefi smiled. "Yes, you in the back."

"Kira Monroe, Deutsche Presse-Angentur. Could you comment on NATOs decision to admit both Belarus and Ukraine, against Russian objections?"

ALSO BY RORI BLEU

Pineapple Meringue

Imprisoned Hearts

Port of London

Dani's Masquerade

Black Tulips

Ajei's Destiny

Porta Aeternum

The Queen's Heart

Syn *with Matthew Forester*

Echoes and Illusions *with Rosie Chapel*

Evie's War *with Rosie Chapel*

Vindicta *with Rosie Chapel*

Corrupt Covenant *with Rosie Chapel*

The Sela Helsdatter Saga *with Rosie Chapel*

A Flip of The Coin - Book One

Conceived Chaos - Book Two

Odin's Bane - Book Three

Valhalla's Doom - Book Four

Arcane Alchemy - Freya's Fate - *A Helsdatter Saga Novella*

ALSO BY ROSIE CHAPEL

<u>Historical Fiction</u>

The Hannah's Heirloom Sequence
The Pomegranate Tree - Book One
Echoes of Stone and Fire - Book Two
Embers of Destiny - Book Three
Etched in Starlight - Prequel
Hannah's Heirloom Trilogy - Compilation — e-book only

Prelude to Fate
Legacy of Flame and Ash

The Nettleby Trilogy (WW1 Novellas)
A Guardian Unexpected - Book One
Under the Clock - Book Two

Evie's War *with Rori Bleu*
Vindicta *with Rori Bleu*
Corrupt Covenant *with Rori Bleu*

The Sela Helsdatter Saga *with Rori Bleu*
A Flip of The Coin - Book One
Conceived Chaos - Book Two
Odin's Bane - Book Three
Valhalla's Doom - Book Four
Arcane Alchemy - Freya's Fate

<u>Regency Romances</u>

The Linen and Lace Series

Once Upon An Earl - Book One

To Unlock Her Heart - Book Two

Love on a Winter's Tide - Book Three

A Love Unquenchable - Book Four

A Hidden Rose — Book Five

The Daffodil Garden

The Unconventional Duchess

Rescuing Her Knight - *the de Wiltons:* Book One

Elusive Hearts - *An Unexpected Romance*: Book One

His Fiery Hoyden

A Regency Christmas Double

Fate is Curious

A Christmas Prayer *with Ashlee Shades*

Luck be a Pirate

The Highwayman's Kiss

The Lady's Wager

Winning Emma

A Love Impossible

Unravelling Roana

Love Kindled

Moonbeams and Mistletoe

<u>Fairy Tale Romance</u>

Chasing Bluebells

<u>Contemporary Romances</u>

Of Ruins and Romance

All At Once It's You

Cobweb Dreams

Just One Step

His Heart's Second Sigh

<u>Dystopian Romance</u>

Echoes & Illusions *with Rori Bleu*

www.ingramcontent.com/pod-product-compliance
Lightning Source LLC
Chambersburg PA
CBHW070359200726
48294CB00003B/998